HERO'S WELCOME

"You!" the trapper snarled at Skye Fargo. "You lousy stinking two-bit hero."

"You're making a mistake . . ." Fargo said softly, trying to calm the man down.

"No mistake I'd be making, or my name's not Terrence O'Shaugnessey," the trapper said hotly, and Fargo took a step backward as the trapper hit him, throwing him off balance, and seized him as they fell together onto the ground.

O'Shaugnessey was as lithe and strong as a cat—and he had one thing a cat didn't have. He had a knife, and it was out, inches from Skye's throat.

The Trailsman decided it was time to stop the blarney—and the butchery. . . .

BLAZING NEW TRAILS
WITH THE ACTION-PACKED
TRAILSMAN SERIES
BY JON SHARPE

THE
TRAILSMAN
133

SAGE
RIVER
CONSPIRACY

by

Jon Sharpe

A SIGNET BOOK

SIGNET
Published by the Penguin Group
Penguin Books USA Inc., 375 Hudson Street,
New York, New York 10014, U.S.A.
Penguin Books Ltd, 27 Wrights Lane,
London W8 5TZ, England
Penguin Books Australia Ltd, Ringwood,
Victoria, Australia
Penguin Books Canada Ltd, 10 Alcorn Avenue,
Toronto, Ontario, Canada M4V 3B2
Penguin Books (N.Z.) Ltd, 182-190 Wairau Road,
Auckland 10, New Zealand

Penguin Books Ltd, Registered Offices:
Harmondsworth, Middlesex, England

First published by Signet, an imprint of New American Library,
a division of Penguin Books USA Inc.

First Printing, January, 1993
10 9 8 7 6 5 4 3 2 1

The first chapter of this book previously appeared in *Kentucky Colts*, the one
hundred thirty-second volume in this series.

 REGISTERED TRADEMARK—MARCA REGISTRADA

Printed in the United States of America

The Trailsman

Beginnings . . . they bend the tree and they mark the man. Skye Fargo was born when he was eighteen. Terror was his midwife, vengeance his first cry. Killing spawned Skye Fargo, ruthless, cold-blooded murder. Out of the acrid smoke of gunpowder still hanging in the air, he rose, cried out a promise never forgotten.

The Trailsman they began to call him all across the West: searcher, scout, hunter, the man who could see where others only looked, his skills for hire but not his soul, the man who lived each day to the fullest, yet trailed each tomorrow. Skye Fargo, the Trailsman, the seeker who could take the wildness of a land and the wanting of a woman and make them his own.

1860, New Dublin, in what is now the state of Montana . . . a town turned upside down, where loyalty is betrayal, and a man's face makes him a hero or a corpse.

1

There. He saw it again. A flicker of movement in the stand of yellow pine on the hillside. That made two of them, he thought. And if he had spotted two, there were probably a hundred. Blackfoot, creeping down the forested slope. Maybe more than a hundred.

Without reining in his Ovaro, the tall man turned in his saddle and glanced back at the supply train following him. Two-dozen mule-drawn mountain wagons lumbered in the deep ruts cut through the bunchgrass of the rolling plain, under the low, sullen clouds. On the driver's seats were sharp-eyed men, surly, quiet, strange, hunched against the cold, stiff wind that blew out of the north into their faces. A dozen more men of the same kind rode beside the wagons. Sixty men all together.

Skye Fargo cursed inwardly. Why the hell had he taken this job anyway, leading this batch of toughs through bad Indian country? He turned back around in his saddle and rode a few more paces, glancing at the hillside again, reckoning chances.

Another movement. Subtle. But it was there. He sighed. The perfect spot for an ambush lay just ahead, where two gentle wooded slopes pinched the plains. The wagon train was heading for that narrow passage, and Fargo had no doubt that the trees on either side were swarming with armed Blackfoot.

Fargo turned and signaled one of the outriders to approach. The man rode up—a burly bearded fellow.

Fargo remembered his name was Willie. He was one of the few of these taciturn men whose name Fargo knew, even after three weeks on the trail. As far as he could make out, Willie seemed to be the foreman of the group.

"Indians in the trees," Fargo said quietly. Willie's brow darkened with questions, but no fear. He nodded but didn't answer. "A lot of them," Fargo continued. "Pass the word back. On my signal, we'll circle and stand ready to fight."

Willie nodded again and fell back. Fargo slowed the pace of the train and glanced back from time to time. He hoped that as the message was passed from man to man nothing would look suspicious to the watching Indians. If the Blackfoot suspected that they had been sighted, they would spring their ambush early, swooping down on the wagons as they rode strung out across the plain. Fargo watched as they drew nearer to the narrow passage. If they got too close to the gap . . .

Here goes, he said to himself as he suddenly put the spur to the Ovaro and turned him hard about. The first wagon followed, turning off the track and into the rough bunchgrass. The driver laid his whip across the backs of the mules as they came around. In two minutes the wagon train had doubled back and formed a tight circle, back ends facing out, mule teams angled to the inside, horses tethered inside the safety of the large inner circle. They'd lose fewer of their mounts this way than if they used them to form part of the barrier. Also, the tight line of wagons would be harder for the Indians to breach.

Fargo rode about, giving orders. But the men seemed to know exactly what to do. They moved quickly and efficiently. Hell, they were lousy companions at the campfire, but they sure could ride a wagon train. Fargo hoped they'd be good Indian fighters as well, as he dismounted and tied the Ovaro. Willie approached with several of the other men.

"So, where's the redskins?" one red-haired man said roughly.

"They're out there," said Fargo, pointing. "Behind the trees. But they've lost the advantage of surprise. They're trying to decide if they can risk attacking us now that we've circled."

"I don't see none," said the redhead, craning his neck to peer at the slopes.

"Well then, why don't you walk over there and take a closer look?" Fargo said. "Then come back, minus your red scalp, and tell us what you saw."

The man shot an angry look at Fargo and stalked away.

"Just how long do we have to sit here, Fargo?" Willie asked.

"A few hours," Fargo said, glancing at the trees. "Maybe more. The Blackfoot are masters of the surprise attack. Right now they're pissed as hell that we spotted them. They'll wait until they think we've relaxed our guard. Or else they'll withdraw until we move on again."

"We're losing time," protested Willie. "We're supposed to be in New Dublin by nightfall." Several of the men nodded and muttered.

"Better late than never," said Fargo, walking away. Damn, he thought. Damn bunch of ingrates.

He paced around the inside of the circle of wagons and watched the men. They were loading rifles, checking their ammunition, stropping their knife blades. None of them looked up or caught his gaze as Fargo walked by, but he could feel their eyes on his back as he passed. A tough bunch, trail-hardened professionals, every last one of them. Fargo had seen the type before, but never in such a large group.

Why were these men all together on this wagon train? It was a question that had bothered him for three weeks on the trail from Denver City. Most of the wagon trains heading west were full of land-hungry

11

men, wiry women, and silent children, settlers hoping to make a new life.

But these men were not settlers. They were loners. The type that were usually mountain men, prospectors, soldiers . . . or bandits. It didn't make sense.

Fargo sighed and climbed into one of the wagons. He settled himself onto bags of grain, propped open the canvas flap at the rear, and lay back to rest, keeping an eye on the slopes.

The chalky sky overhead was pressing downward, touching the tops of the bare bluffs in the distance. The cold, moist wind flapped the canvas. Snow wind, Fargo thought. There would be snow by morning. Nothing moved on the wooded hillsides.

Waiting, he thought. It was one of the most important skills for survival in the wild. Wait for the Indians to make a move. Wait for the deer to wander into the glade. Wait for your horse to whinny. Wait for darkness so no one can see you. Wait for a man to betray his thoughts in his words or in his face. Wait until you know exactly what's what. Then act.

Fargo smiled at his thoughts. Then why the hell hadn't he waited for a better offer, he asked himself. Damn. Three weeks back he'd been at loose ends between jobs and sitting in a bar in Denver City when an Irishman with a lot of money asked him to do a job. Easy job. Take sixty men in a wagon train north to a place called New Dublin, right at the forty-ninth parallel on the Canadian border. Half the money up front. The rest on arrival. Fargo had pocketed the first thousand dollars and set out.

But it had been a strange trip. Full of silences and questions with no answers. The men didn't talk to him. They fell silent when he approached their campfires. The wagons were full of supplies, food, and ammunition. A lot of ammunition. Boxes of rifles and bullets and an entire wagon full of gunpowder. Fargo had asked Willie about that and about New Dublin.

But Willie was buttoned up tight. And finally Fargo gave up questions and withdrew to his own fire, his own company. Now he was waiting. Waiting to find out what the hell was going on. Waiting for Blackfoot to attack.

Fargo sighed and stretched. Outside he heard the clatter of pans. The cook was fixing the midday meal. He rose to make sure they weren't letting down their guard. The warm smell of bacon, coffee, and bread wafted inside the wagon and drew him out.

Most of the men were lined up at the campfire holding their tin plates for the cook to load up. Fargo checked the wagons. At least a dozen armed men were on guard, watching the plains and the hillsides beyond. Fargo joined the line at the fire and found himself behind Willie.

"No Indians yet," Fargo said, hoping to draw out the man. Willie glanced up and nodded. "By the way, what's your full name, Willie?" Fargo asked. "I never thought to ask."

"O'Brien," Willie muttered.

"Willie O'Brien," Fargo repeated, noting the bit of brogue in the man's accent. "Now that's an Irish name if I ever heard one. How long have you been in America?"

Willie darted him a black look and turned his back. Fargo sighed and shrugged. Hopeless, he thought, as he took his plate of food and returned to the wagon. Now what was taking those Blackfoot so long to make up their minds?

The attack came late in the afternoon, when the clouds had darkened from chalk to gray. Fargo had just climbed out of the wagon to stretch his legs when he caught sight of a long line of movement along the edge of the trees.

"This is it!" he shouted. "Take your positions and fire as soon as they're in range!" The men around

13

him, many of whom were napping or playing cards, jumped to their feet and grabbed their rifles. Fargo checked his Colt and his Sharps rifle, touched the long knife strapped around his ankle, and vaulted onto the driver's seat and rolled into the wagon. He quickly pulled back the canvas for a better view. Two other men joined him, a skinny fellow and the redhead who had taunted him earlier.

"There're your Indians," Fargo said quietly, as he positioned the barrel of his Sharps on the top of the edge of the wagon and watched grimly as the Blackfoot emerged from the edges of the woods at the base of both hills. The redheaded man said nothing, but pressed his lips tight, his squinting eyes watching the tribe.

"Oo-ee," said the skinny one, patting his long Lehman trade musket. "Got lots of targets for you." He moved the grain sacks and a barrel around to give himself better cover.

Fargo bent over and took a sighting on the approaching Blackfoot. The Indians rode forward in a long line, very slowly, not charging yet. They were still outside shooting range. Fargo's sharp eyes picked out the distinctive Blackfoot war bonnets with the feathers sticking straight up on their heads and ermine tails dangling on either side.

His lake-blue eyes narrowed and swept the long line, estimating their number. Close to eighty. Sixty armed men from a fixed position against eighty attacking Indians had a sure chance of winning. Then his hopes sank. This was the first wave, he thought. It was an old Indian trick. Send in some of your force. Then, just when the battle is teetering and the paleface thinks he has a slender chance of winning, send in the rest, screaming bloody murder. It worked every time.

Just as the Blackfoot were within shooting range, one of the braves gave a yell, and the line charged forward. Fargo took aim at a strong buck and squeezed the trigger. The Indian spun and fell, disappearing under the hooves of the oncoming horses. As Skye slipped another cartridge into the Sharps, the redhead got one. The skinny man missed and swore. Fargo heard rifle reports from the other wagons. Several more Indians dropped. The men were good shots, that was for sure. Maybe they had a chance of getting through this.

Fargo ducked as a shot zinged by his head, and he raised his rifle again, sighting an Indian in a war bonnet. He shot low, aiming for the belly, and the Indian slumped forward as the horse slowed and fell back into the oncoming line. Fargo slipped another cartridge into the rifle and then quickly drew his Colt.

As they neared, the Blackfoot suddenly turned and circled the wagons. Fargo watched as they passed, an endless blurred parade of bronzed and muscled warriors, whooping, braids flying and rows of shell necklaces dancing against their chests. Their painted buffalo hide shields were strapped on their arms. Most had rifles. But the bows were no less deadly. Fargo popped up and shot two more in close succession. The redhead winged a third.

An arrow whizzed by and tore through the canvas. Several more struck with a thud against the wooden back of the wagon. A bullet ricocheted, and Fargo heard a scream of agony. He glanced over to see the redhead grasping his side, blood oozing out between his fingers.

"Aw, damn," the skinny man said from behind him, reloading and squeezing off another shot. There was nothing either one of them could do, Fargo thought as he turned his attention back to the Indians. A flash of pain burned his shoulder as an arrow whizzed by, grazing him. Fargo raised the Colt and shot a Blackfoot just as he was ready to let another arrow fly.

Out of the corner of his eye he saw the redheaded

man struggling to sit up. As Fargo and the skinny one picked off more of the Indians, the dying man was painstakingly propping his rifle back up on the wooden wall. An Indian galloped by, leaning out from his saddle, rifle poised, searching for a target. The redhead pulled the trigger at the same moment the Indian fired on him. The rifles exploded simultaneously, and Fargo saw the redhaired man jump once. He didn't move again. Fargo glanced out at the Indian slumped across the back of his pony.

Fargo reloaded again and again, spending his fury on the Indians as they rode by. The skinny man inched up beside him and, pushing aside the dead man, ducked down behind the wooden boot. The skinny man was a good shot and a good soldier, Fargo thought. They timed their shots and reloadings so that one of them was shooting at any moment.

There were many fewer Indians, Fargo noticed, and a lot of bodies lying on the plain. They rode further from the train, their ranks thinned, dashing in for the sure shots.

"Wonder how many of our men are left?" Fargo muttered, half to himself as he followed a moving Indian with his barrel and brought him down.

"We're all good fighters," the skinny man said, reloading and raising the rifle again. Fargo glanced over at him.

"Where'd you learn to fight?" Fargo asked idly.

The other man didn't look at him, but kept his eye on the Indians passing. They weren't shooting much, but were just circling.

"What are they waiting for?" the skinny man said, not answering Skye's question. Fargo sighed inwardly. He wasn't going to find out anything from this one either.

"Seamuse to bring on the next trick," Fargo said. "My guess is those Blackfoot have more warriors still

16

on the hillside. Or maybe they've got something else up those buckskin sleeves."

The answer came almost immediately, as a burning arrow tore through the canvas above their heads, setting the fabric on fire. So, the Blackfoot were going to smoke them out, Fargo thought. He pulled his neckerchief up over his nose and mouth, gesturing for the other man to do the same. They hunkered down, and Fargo raised his Colt, catching a Blackfoot in the throat as he galloped close by. The brave grasped his throat with both hands as it spurted blood, and he slid from his mount.

The Indians redoubled their attack, and between shots Fargo kept an eye on the burning canvas. The Indians were bolder now, coming in closer. He ducked another arrow as it zinged by.

They could hold out for a while under the burning canvas. Usually the canvas just burned right away, leaving the box of wagon intact, still good cover. He wondered how far the fire was spreading, whether it had reached the supply wagons with boxes of rifles and . . .

"Goddamn gunpowder!" Fargo shouted from beneath his neckerchief.

"Damn!" the skinny man said, lurching sideways as a bullet whistled through.

"We can kiss it all good-bye if that blows!" Fargo said, reloading. "Cover me while I go check on it."

He swore and began sliding out onto the driver's seat of the wagon, keeping low. He dropped onto the balls of his feet and ran, bent double.

Stray shots and arrows had wounded several of the mules, who brayed loudly. Inside the circle no one was in sight. All the men had hidden in the wagons and were shooting. Half of the canvas-topped wagons blazed, the red-gold flames bright against the low gray clouds. Black smoke billowed skyward. None of the men had panicked and fled from the wagons, as settlers usually did when the canvas tops caught fire. The Indians counted on that. No, these men were professionals.

A burning piece of canvas had blown onto the grass in the center of the circle. It wasn't much of a fire yet, but Fargo could see it was spreading, and the steady wind would quickly sweep the narrow fire line across the grass circle, heading straight for the tall wooden-sided wagon which held dozens of barrels of gunpowder. He'd need help. Fargo bent down again and ran to one of the wagons that was not on fire. He lifted the canvas side. Five men were inside. One was Willie, who turned to reload. He started, seeing Fargo's face there, his neckerchief over his nose and mouth.

"What the hell?"

"Fire running toward the gunpowder," Fargo shouted. "I need three men to help me."

Willie and two men quickly jumped out. One man caught a stray shot in the calf, and another vaulted down to replace him, as the wounded one dragged himself back into the wagon.

"Come on!" Fargo shouted, removing his buckskin jacket. Willie and the two men did the same as they raced toward the open center of the circle. The greedy flames licked the tufts of dry grass, and they burst into orange flame, then curled and charred black.

The men spread out in a line to face the oncoming fire. Fargo lifted the jacket above his head, advanced, and brought it down onto the burning grass, snuffing out the flames, beating the fire again and again as the black smoke choked him. He leapt aside as a stray arrow whizzed by, continuing to fight the fire. The men beside him beat back the flames as the wind blew stronger. Fargo fell back as the flames roared up again, their heat like a heavy wall. As the wind stiffened and blew the fire toward him, he felt his hair singe and the skin on his face dry and crack.

"Harder!" Fargo yelled. He glanced behind him and saw that the powder wagon was a dozen yards away. The mule team, still hitched to the wagon, was braying and struggling against their traces as the flames neared. There was a chance that the fire would pass under the wagon without igniting the gunpowder, but only if the flames moved fast enough not to catch fire to the wood or heat the powder to ignition. It was a slim chance. But the sweeping flames would cook the mules, he realized as he continued to beat the flames. The fire was gaining, and the narrow band was spreading at the edges, threatening two other wagons and teams.

There was only one thing to do, he realized, but it was a big risk. Just then one of the men spun about and grabbed his shoulder, holding it tight. He staggered over beside one of the wagons. The Indians had sighted them in the center of the circle and were shooting between the wagons, Fargo realized, as the bullets began to rain in on them.

"We'll have to pull in the circle!" Fargo shouted. "Inside the fire line!" He quickly gestured to the three wagons that were now in the line of the advancing fire.

"It'll blow!" Willie shouted, stepping back.

"It'll blow if we don't!" Fargo yelled. "You men take the outside ones. I'll take the powder. Drive 'em right around the fire and close in the circle."

The two men ran for their wagons, and Fargo vaulted toward the powder supply wagon, dodging bullets. Hell. If he had to die, he was going to go out with a big bang on top of one ton of gunpowder. He clambered onto the driver's seat out of the range of fire, the wagon between him and the circling Indians. He seized the leather whip hanging above his head. The fire was a yard or two in front of the mule team. The mules had backed up as far as they could, balking and braying. He'd have to drive the wagon right over the flames.

He glanced over at the other wagons. Willie and the other man had already got their mules moving, skirting around the flames, drawing in toward the center of the protected circle. The other men had seen what was happening, and several of the wagons were being driven inward to adjust the circle of defense. Yellow blasts of gunfire erupted from the backs of the moving wagons as the men inside fired again and again.

The gunpowder wagon was enclosed in the back and unmanned. Fargo realized he'd have to get the team moving fast or risk being stranded beyond the defense line, in which case the Blackfoot would sweep in on him. Fargo heard a crescendo of yells from the Indians as they saw the wagons moving. He brought the whip down on the backs of the mule team. They started forward a step, and then the lead balked. The flames were right at their feet, and they screamed with agony, refusing to step across the fire.

"Damn," he rasped, his voice hoarse from the acrid smoke, and the smell of burning mule hair in his nostrils. Fargo jumped down, noting the wagons pulling away from him, yard by yard. As he ran through the billowing smoke toward the head of the mule team, he could see the Indians riding between and beyond them. Again and again he swung his jacket over his head, beating the flames until a charred path was cleared for the first two mules. All about him he heard the gunfire and the whine of bullets. The men had him well covered, he realized, or else he'd already be a dead man. Then he seized the bridle of the lead mule and tugged.

"Get going, goddamn you!" he shouted. After a moment's hesitation the first mule stepped forward, and the team moved, stepping gingerly onto the charred ground as the wall of fire swept by them on either side. As the first two rows of mules passed the flames, they quickened the pace, eager to be further from the heat, and Fargo watched with relief as the heavy wooden wagon of gunpowder rolled quickly over the burning grasses.

He pulled the wagon into line with the others, closing the gap. The smoke of the fire line rose like a black wall behind the wagon. Fargo removed his bandanna and wiped his face. The sound of gunfire sputtered and then ceased.

Fargo peered around the side of the wagon and saw the Blackfoot in retreat toward the hillside, their whooping calls soon lost in the wind. He counted about twenty. The Blackfoot had lost three-quarters of their number. Fargo wondered how many of the sixty men had been lost. After a few minutes of silence the men began to emerge from the wagons. Fargo sighted Willie.

"That was some fancy rescue work," Willie said, frank admiration in his voice. "There aren't many men on God's earth who'd dare drive a powder keg right over a fire."

"A calculated risk," Fargo said.

"When'll the redskins be back?" Willie asked. "Got any theories on that?"

"Blackfoot don't usually make a full retreat and then return," Fargo said. "They send in a second assault. But . . . that didn't happen." He was silent for a moment as his thoughts raced on. There hadn't been more Indians waiting in the woods, as he had thought. There had been only eighty Blackfoot. And those eighty, seeing that the wagon train had sixty men and was armed, attacked anyway with no reserves. It had been almost a suicide mission. Or an act of desperation. The odds were against them from the start. Blackfoot didn't usually take risks like that, Fargo thought. Something wasn't right here.

"How many did we lose?" Fargo asked.

"I sent a man around to check. We'll know in a minute," Willie said.

"We won't go further tonight," said Fargo. "The Blackfoot don't fight in the dark. But, post a heavy guard anyway and we'll all sleep better. We'll get an early start in the morning and be in New Dublin by noon."

Willie gestured toward a man approaching them.

"How'd we do?" Willie asked.

"Seven wounded. Four dead. One about to be," the man answered and turned away. Now it was Fargo's turn to be admiring. Amazingly few casualties. He gave a low whistle.

"I'd hate to come up against you and your men," Fargo said. "You're damn good fighters." The burly bearded man shrugged.

"We oughta get some dinner on," Willie said. "Where's cookie?"

During the evening, several of the men slapped Fargo on the back or nodded at him across the campfire, subtly acknowledging his rescue of the gunpowder. But nobody wanted to converse. Nobody opened up. Nobody answered any questions. Fargo fell into his bedroll that night just as puzzled as he had been the whole trip.

Fargo rolled over, shook the snow from on top of his bedroll, and slipped out. Overhead the sky was still black, clouded, and starless with a hint of gray dawn appearing in the east. The snow, blue in the darkness, blanketed the camp and the forms of the sleeping men. Cold snaps were severe in this part of the territory, he thought as he pulled up his collar. He watered and fed the Ovaro, then saddled it and led the horse beyond the wagons and mounted. First he rode once around the periphery of the camp. Eight men on guard, none of them sleeping.

"Any trouble?" he asked one as he passed.

"Quiet as a tomb all night," said the man, "except for wolves howling." Fargo nodded and swung the pinto out on a line toward the hillsides where the Blackfoot had hidden the day before. He guided the stallion in long, sweeping loops, and watched the ground carefully, his sharp eyes scanning the white expanse of new snow. Not a track. Not even a dimple. Close to the trees he saw the signs of a track and slid down from the pinto. Wolf, he said to himself as he mounted again.

As he approached the larger of the two slopes, the pine trees rose before him, silent and black, frosted with heavy snow. He rode into the trees, eyes and ears alert, winding up the hill, side to side, examining the ground. Chipmunks. Squirrels. He rode on, slowly ascending. Once the pinto started when a branch faltered, and a load of snow fell with a soft swoosh. Other than that, there was deep silence.

At the top of the ridge Fargo followed a natural pathway down into a wooded valley. The Blackfoot had probably come this way, he thought. Once again he dismounted. He squatted and brushed away the snow across a wide patch of the path. Underneath, in the wet earth, were the soft impressions of moccasined feet and unshod ponies, Indian ponies, traveling both directions. He rode on for several miles more as the sky lightened above him. Elk tracks. Deer. Hungry deer stripping the bark off saplings. But no fresh human tracks. Finally, he turned the pinto around and rode back to camp. By the time he arrived, the yellow fires were blazing and breakfast was almost done.

"We were just beginning to wonder if you'd gone for good," Willie called out as he saw Fargo dismounting. "Any sign of those Indians?"

"They're miles away," Fargo answered. "But let's get a move on now, in case they change their minds. Today every man rides with his rifle and his pistol loaded."

23

Within minutes the wagon train was ready to roll, the men moving efficiently. Fargo started them off, then signaled two of the outriders to check the trees ahead as he rode out a half mile ahead, preceding them through the gap. But the Blackfoot were nowhere to be seen.

Fargo paused at the top of the bluff and looked down into the valley at the town of New Dublin. The buildings were crowded together, backs to a short cliff, as if huddling close in fear. In the front, a wooden wall ran in a half circle, enclosing the town, and even from this distance Fargo's sharp eyes picked out the moving figures of sentries patrolling the top. Animals pens and snow-covered fields surrounded the village beyond the wall.

The Milk River dropped over the cliff in a short fall, partially frozen, the huge icicles like the bars of a cage. At the bottom of the cliff a large waterwheel revolved relentlessly, propelled by the water which flowed inside the layer of ice.

Fargo's eyes narrowed as he surveyed the scene. He'd seen a lot of frontier towns, hundreds of them—towns that clung to rocky mountainsides, towns that sprouted on the plains like a stand of weeds, towns where the pounding of hammers on new lumber drowned out the sound of gunfire, and towns where the only sound was a shutter banging against the side of an abandoned building.

Fargo felt discomfited as he stared down at New Dublin and read its story the way some men read books. The barricade and the guards told him it was a town at war. At war with the Blackfoot, he thought. But something else bothered him. He glanced over the straight streets, storefronts all alike, the broad church in the center and the whitewashed cottages in rows. Order. Everything was in order, as if someone had designed the village for maximum efficiency. It was not like other sprawling frontier towns, which grew haphazardly. New Dublin had the look and the *feel* of a military garrison.

The jangle of the mule traces brought him out of his thoughts as the wagon train caught up to him. Fargo put his spur to the Ovaro and rode down the long sloping trail that led into New Dublin.

As he approached the barricade, the large gate swung open and a short fat man dashed forward. Sighting Fargo, he came to an abrupt halt, astonishment coloring his already florid face.

"You!" he said. "Saints be praised, you're here at last!"

Fargo nodded and touched his hat brim. The man had a thick Irish accent, he noted.

"Got caught by the Blackfoot ten miles out, or we'd have been here yesterday," Fargo said, swinging down off his horse. Fargo took a step forward and extended his hand. "Glad to meet you. My name's . . ."

"No need for introductions," the man protested. "You're our local hero, you know."

Fargo smiled at him. It sometimes surprised him how far the reputation of the Trailsman had traveled the West. Apparently his description and the stories of his many adventures had made it all the way north to this obscure town. "My name's O'Carroll. Seamus O'Carroll of Tipperary. And I am blessed to meet you."

O'Carroll grasped his extended hand and pumped it, over and over, until Fargo finally withdrew it. Willie O'Brien approached and cuffed Seamus O'Carroll. The two men seemed to be old friends.

"I see you've met Seamus," Willie said.

"Met?" O'Carroll responded. "I mean to tell you we've been waiting for this man for two long years now."

"Him?" Willie asked as Fargo raised his eyebrows.

25

"Don't you know who he is?" O'Carroll said, his face coloring.

"A trailsman," Willie answered, turning to look at Skye Fargo. "And a pretty good one at that."

"A trailsman? You're a good-for-nothing pile of rotten potatoes and you've been gone from New Dublin too long," O'Carroll said, teasingly. "Open your eyes, man." O'Carroll leaned over and whispered something into Willie O'Brien's ear. Willie's eyes widened, and he looked Skye Fargo up and down slowly.

"But . . . but . . . his name's Skye Fargo," Willie said to O'Carroll.

"Sure, that's what he'd be telling you, wouldn't he?" Seamus answered.

This was getting a little out of hand, Fargo thought, irritation beginning to replace the pleasant feeling of being flattered. Fargo wanted to get the second installment of his money and be on his way.

"Who's in charge here?" he said sharply to the two men. "Now that I've delivered the wagon train, I'd like to be getting on with it." The two men jumped.

"Be getting on with it!" O'Carroll said, delightedly. "Cool as a cucumber in God's garden! Just like that. Deliver the wagon train and get on with it, like it was nothing!"

Fargo sighed. This was really annoying. He reached over and grasped Seamus O'Carroll's collar.

"Look, O'Carroll," Fargo said, drawing his face near so that they were nose to nose, "I've ridden a long way. I'm tired. Who's in charge here?" Seamus's face flushed and Fargo released him. O'Carroll backed away, sudden fear on his face.

"Of course, sir. Begging your pardon for shooting off my mouth like that," Seamus said. "You'd be wanting Bill O'Hagan. I'll take you right to him."

Willie O'Brien returned to the wagon train as O'Carroll led him through the gate. The men on top whistled and shouted greetings. Fargo waved back.

26

Despite appearances, it was certainly a friendly town. Two young women, bundled against the cold, were emerging from a dry goods store and sighted him walking with O'Carroll. They stopped and pointed at him as he walked by. He tipped his hat to them and they giggled and hid their faces in their fur muffs.

O'Carroll led him to the door of a storefront with no sign and went inside. Fargo followed, stamping the snow off his boots and glancing about the room. Two desks stood against the wall and a dozen mismatched chairs clustered about a table. A map of Canada and a colored drawing of St. Patrick were tacked to one wall. At one of the desks a thin angular man with slicked down dishwater blond hair sat reading a page on which Fargo could see columns of figures. The man continued to read for a few moments after they entered, and then he turned slowly around. When his eye caught Fargo's face, he jumped to his feet.

"You're here!" he stammered and his mouth hung agape. His eyes, set close together on either side of a bulbous red nose, registered astonishment. "We weren't expecting you so soon!"

"According to my contract, I was supposed to arrive yesterday," Fargo pointed out. "And we would have, but Blackfoot Indians ambushed us."

"Ambush?" the man said.

"No surprise to you, I imagine. You must have a lot of Indian attacks here," Fargo said, thinking of the barricade around the town.

"Those red devils would never dare attack New Dublin," the man said, pride edging his voice. "They never have and they never will." Fargo felt the questions rise in him. If not for Indians, what was the barricade for? No need to ask the man flat out, he decided. There might be more here than simple questions could answer. O'Carroll excused himself and left.

"Sorry I didn't introduce myself," Fargo said, extending his hand. "The name's Skye Fargo." The tall

27

man grasped his hand and shook it, a smile on his thin lips, his head nodding.

"Is that what you'd be calling yourself? And you're talking with an American accent," he said. "You have a reputation for cleverness and I think it's well-earned. Well, it's an honor to meet you now, Mr. Skye Fargo." Fargo felt confused at the words and wondered if the man wasn't a little muddleheaded.

"You must be Bill O'Hagan." The man shook his head vehemently.

"No, alas. The great Mr. O'Hagan is gone for the day to check on . . . things." He gave Fargo a conspiratorial wink. "Mr. O'Hagan is an important man. I'm only Tom Fitzgerald. From the Fitzgeralds around Limerick."

"Is everyone in New Dublin Irish?" Fargo asked. Fitzgerald gave a hearty laugh.

"Now that's a good one," he said, wiping the tears from his eyes. Fargo watched him, wondering what the joke was. "Is everyone . . . in this . . . town . . . Irish?" Fitzgerald repeated, between chuckles. Then he abruptly stopped and peered into Fargo's face. "That's a serious question you'd be asking is it?"

Fargo nodded. Was the man mad? He watched Fitzgerald's face closely as the man considered the question, his face twisted with thought.

"We've always heard you're a man who asks the right questions," Fitzgerald said in a low voice. "And that is a timely question, a subtle question, a question that could mean our life and our death. Now that I'm thinking of it, there is a man in New Dublin who is not Irish. A photographer by the name of Oscar Wyndham."

"Interesting," Fargo said noncommitally, eager to change the subject, get his pay, and get the hell out of this insane asylum.

"Would you be telling me that you'd be thinking

Oscar Wyndham is . . . a spy?" Fitzgerald whispered. The man was stark-raving mad, Fargo decided.

"I doubt it," Fargo reassured him. "Look, when is Bill O'Hagan coming back?" Fargo said to change the subject. "I'm looking to get paid."

"I'll bet you are," Fitzgerald said, a big smile lighting his face. "Mr. O'Hagan's making a wonderful party for you."

"I'm not interested in a party," Fargo said. This was going too far.

"I wouldn't be blaming you," Fitzgerald said. "If I was in your shoes, I'd be more interested in the girl."

"And what girl is that?" Fargo asked.

"Why Bernadette. O'Hagan's youngest daughter," Fitzgerald said. "Now that you're here, your wedding will be set for day after tomorrow."

2

"My wedding?" Fargo repeated incredulously. "There must be some mistake."

"Oh, it's no mistake Mr. O'Hagan would be making," Fitzgerald assured him. "Bill O'Hagan never makes a mistake. Bernadette's a good-looking colleen, even if she is a handful of trouble. And a bit of a redheaded rebel to boot. O'Hagan's been wanting to make this match ever since he heard of your many heroic deeds and reputation. Soon as he knew you were coming to New Dublin, he made the arrangements."

"Look," Fargo said. "I'm not marrying this Bernadette . . .

"Oh, Mr. O'Hagan predicted you might go and say that once you arrived," Fitzgerald said. "We've heard it's hard to tie you down. But you can't go disappointing Mr. O'Hagan like that. After all, you gave your promise."

"What are you talking about?" Fargo shouted. "I never agreed to marry anybody! You've got me confused with some other man."

"Oh, you'd be having the gift of blarney, wouldn't you? Well, the marrying jitters are a natural thing for a man," Fitzgerald said. Fargo realized that arguing with Tom was like talking to a stone wall. Well, he'd shut up and bide his time. When O'Hagan came back he'd reason with him, explain the mistake, get the thousand dollars owed him, and get the hell out.

"Never mind," Fargo said. He glanced out the window and noticed how dark it had become. The snow clouds had gathered again, and a few flakes were falling in the early dusk. "It's getting late. Where's the hotel?"

"Bill O'Hagan wouldn't allow a hotel in New Dublin, that's for certain," Fitzgerald said as he rose and put on his sheepskin coat. "But we can drop in on Maureen O'Shea. She has a nice room she lets out sometimes. Yes, she'd like to look you over since you're going to become one of the family. You might have heard Maureen was widowed last summer, poor thing."

"I didn't hear anything about it," Fargo said hotly. "And I . . ."

"Of course, I've heard all the stories about you keeping busy chasing around the old country blasting away at those rotten landlords," Fitzgerald said as he locked the office door behind them and led the way through the gently falling snow. "You don't have time for keeping up on the news from New Dublin."

Fargo shook his head in frustration. It was useless talking to Fitzgerald, he realized. And he was about to spend a long winter's night in a nice room with a widowed old lady in a godforsaken town of Irish lunatics on the Canadian border. Great.

"What do you mean, O'Hagan won't allow a hotel in town?" Fargo asked as they made their way through the deserted street. "Is he the king here? Or just the mayor?"

Fitzgerald's laugh was like a short bark.

"Bill O'Hagan made this town," Fitzgerald said. "Thanks to him, we're all here, and we're glad of it every day of our lives. We owe Mr. O'Hagan a big debt, so if he doesn't see fit to be putting any hotels or eating establishments or banks in town, then we owe it to him to go along."

"No banks in town either?" Fargo said. "How do you handle finances?"

"Mr. O'Hagan and I take care of all the accounts."

Fargo nodded thoughtfully to himself as they walked, the fresh snow squeaking beneath their boots. Clearly if O'Hagan held the town purse strings, he would have Fargo's thousand dollars. He would have to hope O'Hagan was honest as well as reasonable.

"Who's the sheriff?"

"Why, there wouldn't be any crime in New Dublin," Fitzgerald answered. "Mr. O'Hagan sees to that. Here we are."

They stopped before a large whitewashed cottage with a stone chimney. Mixed with the smoke coming out of the chimney was the warm odor of meat stew. An evening with an old widow might not be so bad if she was a good cook, thought Fargo. Golden light streamed from small lace-curtained windows. Willie rapped on the thick wooden door.

"Who'd be there?" a muffled woman's voice said from inside.

"Tom Fitzgerald."

"Get you gone!" she said. "How many times do I have to tell you I'm not interested in you coming acourting!"

Fargo smiled to himself. So Tom was chasing the widow, was he. And unsuccessfully.

"Maureen. I'd be bringing you a guest for the night. Somebody to rent your room!"

The immediate sound of a bolt being drawn was their answer, and the door swung slowly open.

"A guest you say?" Maureen answered.

Fargo started at her appearance. No wonder Fitzgerald was chasing her. Maureen flicked her large brown eyes impatiently over Fitzgerald, and then her gaze came to rest on Fargo. Her eyes, rimmed by full dark lashes, grew large, and her dark brows, dramatic against her pale skin, shot up in surprise. Then she very slowly smiled, as if she knew him already, and

Fargo could almost taste her curved sensuous mouth, like a sweet pink blossom.

She flicked her thick brown wavy hair back from her shoulders and adjusted her woven shawl, letting one side fall and his eyes lingered on her creamy neck and the high, swelling mounds of her full breasts which pushed up above the neckline of her tight plaid woolen dress. With one hand, she played with the front buttons. He imagined them bursting open and glanced up into her eyes. She had noted the direction of his gaze.

He was surprised by the suddenness of his reaction to Maureen O'Shea, an overwhelming desire to possess her white softness. He felt himself harden immediately in anticipation of the long pleasurable winter night ahead and watched as her gaze explored his eyes, lingered on his broad shoulders, and traveled down his long lean muscular body. He unbuttoned his coat as if preparing to enter and let it fall open, enjoying the widening of her eyes as she glimpsed his muscular thighs and his long, hard readiness, obvious beneath his Levi's.

Fitzgerald cleared his throat.

"Can we come in now, Maureen?" he asked plaintively. Clearly Fitzgerald hadn't even noticed what had passed between him and Maureen, Fargo thought.

"I've only got room for one," she said, stepping aside to let Fargo pass by and then shutting the door on Fitzgerald. Fargo heard him swearing as he moved off down the street. Fargo slipped out of his coat, and she took it, hanging it on a peg. His eyes surveyed the room in an instant.

The wide stone fireplace took up one wall, and over the crackling fire cast-iron pots on hooks emitted savory steam. To one side stood a gleaming dark wood table, chairs, and cupboards. A rocking chair stood in a corner beside a window, and balls of yarn filled a basket on the floor. A thick bearskin rug lay across the wide wooden planks of the floor. Through a doorway Fargo glimpsed the end of an iron bedstead.

"I appreciate your letting me stay the night," Fargo said, turning toward her.

"Anything I can do for the cause," she said softly, her eyes smiling at his.

"And what cause is that?" he asked, smiling back.

"Keeping a big man like you in fighting form could be one cause," she said, her eyes twinkling.

He shrugged and smiled. Funny answer.

"My name's Skye Fargo," he said. "Some folks call me the Trailsman."

"Skye Fargo," she said, as if chewing the name. "Skye Fargo. Very nice name to travel under. I know all about you already."

Fargo grinned.

"Yeah? Like what?"

"I've heard the stories about your bravery, your cleverness, your dedication. And folks say you've killed more men than anyone can count. All for the cause."

"What's this cause you keep referring to?" Fargo asked. "I don't kill men for a cause. I kill them when I don't have a choice. When it's them or me."

"Of course," she breathed. "That's a cause. And I've heard stories about your . . . your exploits." Maureen was watching him carefully, her fingers idly playing with the top button on her tight dress. The golden firelight danced across the curves of her cleavage.

"Really?" Fargo muttered, his eyes on her. She blushed and looked away toward a kettle boiling on the fire.

"But, I'd be forgetting myself now," she said briskly. "You must be tired and ready to get out of those clothes and wash up. Why don't you go on into that room and I'll bring you in some hot water in a moment."

Fargo was in the bedroom taking off his shirt when

he heard her enter. He turned and she stopped, the wash basin and pitcher in hand. Maureen's eyes widened as she surveyed his broad shoulders and chest. He smiled at her expression.

"You're stronger and more handsome than I even imagined," she said, placing the basin and pitcher on a side table. She smiled bewitchingly over her shoulder as she turned back toward the outer room. Fargo followed her and leaned against the doorway.

"And what kind of stories have you heard about me?" he asked. Maureen turned back to see him standing there. She very slowly parted her pink lips before she spoke.

"Oh, about the men you've killed. The battles you've won. The women you've . . ." her voice trailed off as she looked up at him.

"And, do you believe those stories?" he asked her, stepping closer.

"Let's just say I'd . . . I'd like to find out if they're true," she answered.

Fargo felt the throbbing between his legs as he pulled her near him and bent over to kiss her deeply. Her mouth was warm and welcoming, sweet and yet insistent. Skye held her head between his hands, running his fingers through her thick dark curls as their mouths drank one another. She was panting when he pulled away and nibbled on her silken neck, his mouth exploring downward over the soft swellings above her neckline. He ran his hands lightly over her constrained breasts and felt her fumbling with the buttons as he gently nuzzled her.

"Oh, yes," she murmured. "It's been so long." He kissed her again deeply, her mouth even warmer, more open to him, more hungry. The buttons came loose one by one and she slipped the dress off. It fell down around her, and he felt her loosening her petticoats too. He moved his hands and found her in a tight lacy corset, her breasts pushed upward, the

35

nipples covered by transparent white lace. He kissed her neck and cleavage, gently nuzzling the lace downward to expose a delicate pink nipple, crinkled with desire. He took it gently between his lips and sucked, then flicked his tongue rapidly over it.

"Oh . . . oh," she moaned. "Oh, yes, more." He let his hands slowly edge downward, along the dramatic curve of her waist to the top of her bloomers. He gently eased them downward over her smooth hips, and she wriggled out of them as they fell around her ankles. As she clung to him, he moved his mouth to the other breast. His hands lightly, teasingly, explored the ruffled bottom edge of the corset, the garters holding her stockings, the silkiness of the skin on her inner thigh, the short curly nap delicately brushing against the warm folded wetness of her.

Maureen moaned and her knees weakened. He caught her against him and lowered her slowly onto the bearskin rug. Then he stood over her as he unbuttoned his shirt and removed it. Maureen lay stretched out before him on the bearskin, all curves and lace, her long dark curly hair strewn across the fur, her nipples peeking out of the lace corset, her shapely thighs apart and inviting.

Fargo smiled down at her and undid his Levi's, removing them and his shorts in one motion. She blinked when she saw his erection, and he lowered himself down between her legs.

"Yes," she said. "Please."

He didn't wait, but took her knees and pulled her toward him, opening her legs wider. She reached down and grasped him, gasping and guiding him inside her as he plunged deeply, to the hilt, into her tight wetness.

"Oh God," she screamed. He pumped into her, grinding against her, feeling the wet folds of her against him, her dark portal contracting around him as he plunged again and again in a wild, uncontrollable passion. He reached down and squeezed her buttocks, pushing harder into her as she bucked and moaned. He slowed a little, holding back as he heard her screams mounting in pitch.

"Yes, yes, now," she screamed, and as she shuddered he felt the explosion gathering in the base of him as he gave it to Maureen, shooting up into her as the firelight shattered into golden splinters and the room whirled.

"The stories were true," she sighed after a while, turning to look him in the face, the firelight golden in her eyes.

"We've only just started," he said smiling, tickling her thigh. He let his hand wander back to her wetness and massaged her gently as she lay back, panting. In a few moments he was ready again, mounting her and thrusting, more slowly, until they came again, with less urgency. Then he kissed her eyelids and face as she lay underneath him.

"Does dinner come with the room too?" Fargo asked, after a time, distracted by the smells of the cooking food.

"Oh!" she said, pushing him off and jumping up. "My soda bread!" She dashed to the hearth and grasped a pair of iron tongs. He rolled over and took in the sight of her in her corset and garters as she bent over to retrieve the food from the fire. He was ready again by the time she turned back.

"Later," she said, noticing. "Dinner first."

The evening was a confusing kaleidoscope of pleasures, from lovemaking on the wooden table, to the bed, to a warm bath at midnight. Finally, they nestled under the covers, and Maureen fell asleep, her tousled hair a dark cloud on the white pillows. Fargo lay awake listening to the soft hiss of falling snow against the windowpane.

He felt rested, well-fed, rejuvenated. His thoughts

turned to the frustrating conversation with Tom Fitzgerald. Obviously, Fitzgerald had him confused with somebody who was supposed to be coming into town to marry O'Hagan's daughter Bernadette. Well, in the morning he'd straighten it all out with O'Hagan and be on his way.

Then his thoughts turned to the men in the wagon train and all the ammunition, enough for an army. What were they supposed to be doing here? Fitzgerald had said the Blackfoot had never attacked the town. Then what was the barricade all about? He felt his curiosity aroused, like a nagging appetite to be satisfied.

A little snooping around town in the morning, he decided, as he felt sleep overtake him, and the answers to his questions would probably be plain as the nose on his face.

The smell of baking bread awoke him, and he stretched lazily, enjoying the fresh sheets and the warmth of the morning sunlight across the bed. He arose, washed, and dressed quickly.

Maureen was just pouring hot water into the teapot when Fargo emerged.

"Good morning, Redmond," she said brightly.

"What?" he asked. "The name's Skye Fargo."

"Oh, we don't have to play that game this morning," Maureen said, taking a seat at the table and motioning him to join her.

Fargo stood over her, looking down.

"Look, Maureen. Last night was great. One of the best nights I've ever had. Believe me when I tell you that. And also believe that I don't know what the hell you're talking about."

"Redmond, stop playing games," she said petulantly, her dark brows lowering. She put sugar into her tea. Fargo lowered himself into the chair opposite her.

"Who is Redmond?" he asked.

Maureen smiled back at him bewitchingly.

"You are, darling."

Fargo felt himself growing hot. This was like his conversation with Fitzgerald the day before.

"How do you know?" Fargo said.

"Stop it," she said. "You've been in the newspaper every week for months. But we thought you weren't arriving for a few more days."

"What newspaper?" Fargo said. "Have you got a copy?"

Maureen smiled and rose. In moment she returned and handed him a folded paper. He opened it. Across the top was written "The Echo of Erin, The News of New Dublin." She pointed to an item and he read:

IRISH HERO COMES TO NEW DUBLIN . . . All of the town is preparing to give a grand welcome to Ireland's foremost patriot, Redmond O'Keefe. Mr. O'Keefe is widely known for his bravery and derring-do in fighting for the freedom of Ireland. He has been traveling from Erin for a month, making stops to visit our brothers-in-arms in New York and Niagara.

"We are most pleased to be welcoming such an exalted personage to New Dublin," commented Bill O'Hagan. "Coming in our hour of need, the promise of Redmond O'Keefe to help us in our just cause for the good of fair Ireland will long be remembered in history. And I am most proud that he will become my son-in-law."

Redmond O'Keefe is engaged to marry O'Hagan's youngest daughter, Bernadette, who chose not to comment.

Fargo put the paper down on the table.

"Interesting," he said. "But what's it got to do with me? Why do you think I'm Redmond O'Keefe?"

"I know, and the whole town is knowing who you are from that face of yours!" Maureen got up abruptly and opened the cupboard, turned, and tossed a photograph down on the table before him.

It was one of the newfangled kind, the size of a calling card. Staring back at him was his own face.

Fargo started. He picked up the photograph and studied it carefully. The man in the picture was a dead ringer for himself: tall, dark-bearded, muscular, with deep, searching eyes. The man wore a dark felt hat and a European-cut jacket. As he scrutinized the picture, he began to see a slight difference in the shape of the man's jawline. But the likeness was close. Damn close. That explained what had been happening ever since he reached New Dublin, he thought. Fitzgerald and even Maureen had thought he was Redmond O'Keefe.

Well, if the real Redmond O'Keefe *was* due in town in a few days, that would clear up matters once and for all. But he didn't want to waste time waiting around. Fargo tossed the photo onto the table, took a swallow of tea, and ate some of the soda bread in thoughtful silence as Maureen watched him.

"You look angry," she said at last.

"I am," he said. "I'm not Redmond O'Keefe and I'm not about to marry this Bernadette O'Hagan."

"She doesn't want to marry you either," Maureen said, smiling and ignoring his first comment. "Bernadette's been carrying on for months about it, kicking and screaming and threatening to run away. But where would she run to?" Maureen poured herself another cup of tea. "Besides, she's a scrawny thing. You need a real woman. Like me."

"Now hold on just a moment . . ." Fargo said.

"And when I tell my father what happened last night, it's for certain he'll see it your way. He doesn't care which one of us you'd be marrying, as long as you are his son-in-law."

"Which one of us who?" Fargo said.

"Us. Me and my sister. You can marry me instead of my sister, Bernadette."

Fargo's head reeled. Oh great. Maureen and Bernadette were sisters, both daughters of O'Hagan. This was getting more complicated by the moment. He rose.

"I think I'll have a look around town," he said, putting on his jacket. Maureen ran over to him and gave him a quick hug.

"Come back soon and there'll be more of what you had last night," she said.

Fargo left hastily. Damn, he thought. And it had been such a fun night.

The fresh snow sparkled in the strong morning sun, already softening in the warm chinook wind which blew against his face. The rhythmic creaking of wood drew his attention, and he noted the waterwheel turning slowly at the foot of the cliff under the spectacular icy falls. He struck out in that direction.

He heard the gurgle of the water running under the ice as he approached the river. A short man carrying a heavy burlap bag hailed him from the doorway of the wooden building. Fargo recognized Seamus O'Carroll and sauntered over.

"How would you be liking our village of New Dublin, Mr. O'Keefe?" Seamus asked. Fargo knew it was useless to protest his identity. Maybe by playing along he could find out what was going on.

"Nice town."

"Come on inside and see our grainery."

Fargo entered and watched as O'Carroll slit open the bag and spread the grain across the huge horizontal stone wheel which turned very slowly, bringing the grain under a second gigantic wheel which slowly crushed it.

"We can grind thirty bags of grain a day," Seamus said proudly. "But tell me now. There's something

41

I've been wondering. Do you think we've got a chance?"

"A chance at what?" Fargo said.

"You know," said O'Carroll, lowering his voice even though there were only the two of them in the grainery. "A chance of winning. A chance of freeing Ireland. I mean to say, man, do you think the British will really roll over for it?"

Fargo nodded slowly, as if considering O'Carroll's questions while his thoughts reeled. Freeing Ireland? British? What was going on?

"We've got a fighting chance," Fargo said at last. It was the best answer he could think of, one that didn't betray the fact that he had no idea what O'Carroll was thinking of.

"A fighting chance!" O'Carroll repeated, slapping his thighs. "Yes, exactly. That's what we Irish have always had. Your being here has given me great courage, Mr. O'Keefe."

"I'll be getting along," Fargo said, eager to be alone to sort out his thoughts.

"Good day to you," Seamus answered with a nod.

Fargo pushed out of the grainery door and walked along the street, hardly acknowledging the greetings of the men and women he passed in the street.

Why would O'Carroll be talking about having a chance to free Ireland? Ireland was thousands of miles away. And what did he mean, would the British roll over for it? Fargo pondered as he walked along until a sudden flash of a familiar face brought him up short.

He stopped and peered through the shop window at the photograph of Redmond O'Keefe on display among the bottles of colored liquids. A green ribbon was wound around the edges of the photo, the same one he had seen at Maureen's.

Fargo shrugged and moved on, then paused at the next window where the same photo was on display, this time framed in heavy gold with a hand-lettered sign reading NEW DUBLIN WELCOMES REDMOND O'KEEFE. By the time he had walked the length of the main street, he had seen the image in dozens of windows.

As Fargo stood looking at one display, he wondered if anyone in town had ever met Redmond O'Keefe. If a man has your face, he thought, it would be prudent to know something about him. Just then a shopkeeper, drying his hands on a towel, came out of the store.

"Why, Mr. O'Keefe," he exclaimed, "welcome to New Dublin! Allow me to introduce . . ."

"Never mind," Fargo said, cutting him off. The shopkeeper fell silent. "Answer a question for me. Where did you get this photograph?"

"Why . . . is there something wrong?" the man asked, looking worriedly at the display. "Oscar Wyndham, the photographer, has been selling your picture all over town. His gallery is just down the street."

"Thanks," Fargo snapped and moved off. Maybe he could find out something about Redmond O'Keefe from Oscar Wyndham. The name rang a bell. Then he remembered that Tom Fitzgerald had mentioned Wyndham as the only man in New Dublin who wasn't Irish. Well, that made two good reasons to pay a call on Wyndham, Fargo decided.

"No, of course I didn't take the photograph of you, sir. I only reproduced it. I'm sorry if I've given offense!" Wyndham said, his hands shaking visibly as he adjusted his spectacles and his pale face flushed. "You see," he rushed on, "the *cartes-de-visite* is the latest in photography. Mr. O'Hagan obtained what is called a negative of the photograph, which enabled me to make many copies. If you want the money I earned from selling your image, I will be happy to give it to you . . ."

The little man opened a drawer and reached inside.

"No, I'm not looking for your money," Fargo said.

"Just information. If you didn't take the photograph of Redmond O'Keefe, then you never met the man?"

Oscar Wyndham shut the drawer and looked up at him curiously.

"No, you and I have never met. But you must remember who took your photo, Mr. O'Keefe. After all, you were there." He smiled shyly at his attempt at a joke, then smoothed down the thinning wisps of pale blond hair on his pate.

"I wasn't there," Fargo explained. "I am not Redmond O'Keefe." Oscar Wyndham's pale watery eyes widened as he regarded the tall man looming before him. For the first time, someone in New Dublin seemed to hear and understand what he was saying, Fargo thought.

The photographer reached under the counter and brought out one of the photographs of O'Keefe and glanced at it, at Fargo, and at the photo again.

"Of course you're not," Wyndham concluded. "Remarkably similar. Remarkably. Hair, face, beard, even your build." He placed the photograph on the counter, removed his spectacles and began to buff them on his vest. "But the jaw is quite different. And something in the eyes. Not the same man at all. But, if you're not Redmond O'Keefe, who are you?"

"Name's Skye Fargo."

"That name's familiar, but I can't quite place it. No, wait. Are you the one they call the Trailsman?"

Fargo nodded.

"Got a good reputation," Wyndham said, replacing his spectacles. "So now, what can I do for you, Mr. Fargo? Want a real portrait made of you? We have tintypes or *cartes-de-visite* . . ."

"Just looking for information," Fargo said. "How long have you been in this town?"

"Too long," said Wyndham with a sigh. "Six months ago, I thought I'd try the West. On the Oregon Trail I got held up at gunpoint. Lost all my cash but not my cameras." Wyndham gestured toward the two large cameras that stood in the middle of the room, opposite a velvet chair, a palm, and a painted backdrop with heavy drapes on either side. "So, I hitched aboard the next wagon train and ended up here. But this is the strangest town I've ever set foot in, and as soon as I can scrape together some money, I'm heading back east."

"How do you mean, the town is strange?" Fargo asked.

"Well, for one thing, every single body in it is Irish. I mean, I don't have anything against Irish people. In fact I like them. They're good customers. But I've never seen a town in America where everybody is all from one place."

"Yeah, that struck me too," said Fargo. "But what else?"

"Well, they all stick together so darned much," Wyndham said. "In fact it's a real relief to have a stranger walk in, and to get this off my chest. It's been bothering me for a long time. See, there's something going on in this town that I can't quite put my finger on. It's like everybody knows a big secret, but nobody's talking. Whenever I come along, everybody shuts up."

"That's interesting," Fargo said. "I had exactly the same experience with a group of toughs I brought up from Denver with a big wagon train of ammunition."

"The wagon trains! Exactly!" said Wyndham, his voice quavering with excitement. "Those supply wagons have been arriving every week for the last three months. They pull up at the town gate, then drive away east toward the Sage River, and nobody says another word about them. At first I asked a few questions, but everybody looked at me like they were about to kill. So, I shut up."

"Well, something's going on," Fargo said. "I won-

45

der what all this talk is about 'the cause'? Maureen O'Shea kept going on . . ."

"Maureen O'Shea!" Wyndham said, shuddering. "Like a black widow spider. Watch out for her. She's her daddy's tool. As dangerous as a knife edge when she doesn't get what she wants. Let me tell you what she's done to her poor sister."

"Bernadette?" Fargo asked.

"Why in the six months I've been here," Wyndham said, his eyes alight, clearly enjoying the opportunity to share his gossip, "that little Bernadette has had two suitors. But Maureen moved in on both of them and took them right away, just to shame Bernadette. And then afterward Maureen dropped the boys flat because they weren't good enough for her. Apparently it's been going on for years, even before she was widowed. And she's the apple of her daddy's eye, so he doesn't see any of it. O'Hagan couldn't figure out why he can't marry off Bernadette, so he figured he'd get rid of her sight unseen. That's why he set his sights on you . . . I mean Redmond O'Keefe . . ." Wyndham glanced up at him.

"Yes," Fargo said slowly. "I've run into Maureen already." The little bitch, he added silently.

"Really?" Wyndham shot him a sharp look and then blushed.

"But how do you know all this?" Fargo asked.

"Everyone comes in to have their portrait made. When I'm under the black cloth fiddling with the metal plates, they carry on talking to beat the band. I've heard it all."

Fargo laughed and then grew sober.

"Well, New Dublin is a strange town," Fargo said. "But it's none of my business. I'm clearing out as soon as I can get the thousand dollars that Bill O'Hagan owes me. What's O'Hagan like?"

Oscar Wyndham grew pale.

"O'Hagan?" he murmured, looking about the

empty studio as if afraid of being overheard. "Bill O'Hagan owns this town and everybody in it. What he says, goes. He's the government, the bank, the law, and the court, all rolled into one. Why I've seen men hanged because Bill O'Hagan said they should be. Let's just say I'd stay on Bill O'Hagan's good side if I were you."

"Thanks for the tip," Fargo said. "I'll be seeing you around."

Fargo left Oscar Wyndham's Photography Gallery and headed toward where the Ovaro was stabled. He knew a bad gamble when he saw one and this was it. If he took the pinto and rode out of town now, all he was losing was the thousand bucks he was owed. Sure, that was too bad, but the chances of getting his pay out of O'Hagan looked pretty slim, especially when the truth came out that he'd enjoyed the company of O'Hagan's favorite daughter, Maureen, while engaged to his other daughter Bernadette when he wasn't even Redmond O'Keefe. Of course, he'd like to know about those supply wagons. What was that all about? Well, that was somebody else's problem. It was time to cut his losses and get the hell out.

He took a deep breath and pictured the wide open trail before him, solitary campfires at night, no complications. That would do just fine, he thought as he rounded the corner and entered the stable yard.

A man, a trapper by the look of his moccasins and the fraying fringe across his back, was paying the stable owner. Fargo approached just as the man turned.

"You!" the trapper shouted, looking into Fargo's face. "You lousy, stinking two-bit hero. Why the hell are you bringing your hate into this town? Haven't we got killing enough at home that you don't have to bring it over here too?"

Fargo pulled up short and regarded the man. He was ageless, tough, and wiry, with the look of a man who long lived in the wilds. His battered hat was askew on his head, hanks of black hair hanging down over his shoulders, his deep-socketed eyes wary above haggard and grizzled cheeks.

"You're making a mistake . . ." Fargo said in a low voice to the man. If he could just get to his pinto and ride out quietly . . .

"No mistake I'd be making, or my name's not Terrence O'Shaugnessey," the man said hotly. "I know your kind. I came to this country to get away from you and men like you. I've been here for twenty years, longer than any of you. This is a clean country, a good country, and there's plenty of room for everybody!"

"I agree," Fargo said, "with every word you're saying." He tried to edge around O'Shaugnessey, but the trapper blocked him.

"Don't lie to me, O'Keefe," O'Shaugnessey spat. "I'm sick and tired of the lies in this town. You and Bill O'Hagan have something big up your sleeves. Don't think I don't know what it is. I've seen the camp! And I tell you, the Blackfoot have a right to their land. You are going to do to them what was done to us back in Ireland!"

Fargo thought fast. O'Shaugnessey knew something and thought there was about to be an Indian war. Fargo noticed that the stable owner had taken a keen interest and was watching them carefully. Two other men had rounded the corner and stood watching.

"I'd like to talk to you about all that, O'Shaugnessey," Fargo said, his voice low and calm. "Now why don't we just go off somewhere and . . ."

"I know what kind of talk that is!" O'Shaugnessey shouted. "That's the kind of talk Bill O'Hagan has with men who disagree with him. And that's right before they disappear! Well, there's no one but me in this town that'll dare say that to you, Mr. Redmond O'Keefe. And there's no one but me in this town that'll put an end to this killing!" O'Shaugnessey's black eyes glittered as he crouched down, his hands jabbing the air in front of him.

"I don't want to fight you," Fargo said evenly, backing away. "I've got no quarrel with you."

"Well, I've got one with you," O'Shaugnessey said, lunging forward.

Fargo took a step backward as the trapper hit him, throwing him off balance and seizing him as they fell together onto the ground. O'Shaugnessey was as lithe and strong as a cat. The trapper locked his arm around Fargo's neck, Indian style, and Fargo delivered a hard blow to the man's belly, felt him give a little, and then jammed his right up against the lock, breaking free.

He rolled away, hoping O'Shaugnessey would back off. He noticed that a crowd of men had gathered around them. Just as he was turning back, Fargo heard the whisper of a drawn blade and the jarring impact as the trapper threw himself on him again. Fargo rolled and grabbed his knife arm as the blade descended, stopping it inches from his neck. He held O'Shaugnessey's wavering arm. As strong as the trapper was, Fargo had more power in his biceps, and they both knew it. Fargo looked into the man's eyes.

"You don't want to keep the killing going for no reason," Fargo said quietly. "You're making a mistake." The trapper's eyes took on a troubled look for a brief moment.

Then Fargo felt a sudden jolt as O'Shaugnessey pitched sideways, rolling off of him. Above him, Fargo saw a barrel-chested man with three chins and eyes that were almost lost in his florid puffy flesh.

"Would you be wanting me to kick him again, Redmond?" the man asked, extending his hand to help Fargo up. Fargo refused the hand and got to his feet dusting himself off.

"Welcome to New Dublin," the big man said. "I'm Bill O'Hagan." He motioned to several bystanders and pointed to Terrence O'Shaugnessey, who was just getting to his feet. "Haul this scum off. He's been a thorn in my side for a long time. I'll take the greatest of pleasures in shooting O'Shaugnessey myself. But later."

3

"It's nothing . . . a misunderstanding I've had with O'Shaugnessey," Fargo said, as several men made a grab for the trapper. He struggled in their grasps.

"Nay, you be leaving this turncoat to us," O'Hagan said. "We know the man well. He would be the trouble-making kind, the kind of man who'd not stand for us, who'd not stand for his own kind. There'd be nothing more sorrowful than an Irishman who's lost his love of Erin." O'Hagan paused and gestured to the men holding the trapper. "Be gone with him now. Lock him up good, for I'll be wanting to take care of him later." The men quickly obeyed, as if waiting for O'Hagan's command. "And you now," O'Hagan said to Fargo, "come along with me, Mr. O'Keefe."

"There's been a mistake," Fargo said as he watched the men lead away O'Shaugnessey, who was not going quietly. As they disappeared around a corner, Fargo turned to confront O'Hagan. "I'm not Redmond O'Keefe. The name's Fargo. Skye Fargo."

O'Hagan squinted one eye and looked him up and down, his small eyes narrowing and his triple chins puffing out as he nodded his head.

"Aye, Mr. O'Keefe," he said with a slow smile. "You can call yourself anything you please while you'll be coming to New Dublin. But now you are here among friends and patriots. You'll not be needing those shenanigans."

"I suppose not," said Fargo, slowly with a shrug,

realizing it was useless to protest. Even if he did convince O'Hagan of his real identity, what then? There was no telling what O'Hagan might do. He'd have to pretend to be Redmond O'Keefe. At least for the moment.

"Aye, but I'd be forgetting myself!" O'Hagan said, seizing Fargo's hand. "Welcome officially to New Dublin. It's our Irish heart in America, beating with the blood of patriotism and the blood of all the Fenians! And let me tell you how proud we are to have you here to lead us. The men are all ready and assembled . . . but more talk about that later. Have you seen the town yet?"

"Not really," Fargo answered. The less he said, the less likely O'Hagan would catch on that he wasn't Redmond O'Keefe.

"Well, let me take you for a bit of a walk around and then we'll head home for a wee drop of poteen, a bit of fiddle and jig, and a glimmer of your intended colleen, Mr. O'Keefe. We've got wedding plans to make."

Fargo followed O'Hagan as he moved off down the street. He'd keep his ears open, he decided. In the guise of Redmond O'Keefe, he might find out what was up. And, in any case, he would slip away from the town as soon as possible. Certainly before there could be any more complications. Like a wedding.

Fargo noticed O'Hagan's bandy legs; it was as if the weight of his big girth had forced his knees apart. It gave him a swagger, made all the more intimidating by the constant slow swivel of O'Hagan's head, turning from side to side as he walked along. The man missed nothing, Fargo realized. O'Hagan was not a man to be underestimated.

As they ambled down the street, Bill O'Hagan began to show him the town, pointing out the mill and the waterwheel, various houses, and O'Keefe's portrait in the shop windows. Fargo listened and nod-

52

ded intermittently, his thoughts whirling. He wondered what O'Hagan was planning to do to Terrence O'Shaugnessey.

". . . and this is our wee house," O'Hagan said proudly, drawing up short. The whitewashed cottage with a shingled roof was the largest one in town. Its small windows made the house look as if it squinted suspiciously. A tangle of dead stalks poked through the melting snow in the window boxes. O'Hagan opened the door and motioned Fargo inside.

There was a chill in the air and the large room was lit only by a smoky fire. On the bare stone floor was a heavy dark wood table and rude chairs. The smell of burned food and homemade liquor hung in the air.

"Bernadette!" O'Hagan roared as he slammed the door behind him. "Get yourself down here girl. I'd be bringing your man home to you!"

Bill O'Hagan's voice reverberated through the house, but there was no answer. In the long silence Fargo heard a slight rustle upstairs, and O'Hagan must have heard it too because he swore and threw off his coat, letting it drop onto the floor. He crossed the room quickly and mounted the wooden stairs. Fargo eased himself out of his jacket and looked about for a peg, finding one near the door. Above, he heard O'Hagan's muffled voice, angry, and a woman's voice answering, low.

While he waited Fargo threw another log on the fire and stirred it with the poker, rearranging the logs until the yellow flames leapt up the chimney and the heat blasted his face. When he heard footsteps on the stair, he turned.

Bill O'Hagan had his hand on the girl's shoulder, pushing her downstairs ahead of him. Fargo could see her reluctance in the way she resisted her father and kept her gaze directed at the floor. She was tall, he saw, with long legs and small high breasts. Her green wool dress clung to her willowy form and her long wavy red hair was drawn back in a white ribbon. At the bottom of the staircase, she let go of the banister and clasped her pale hands before her, twisting them nervously, still refusing to look up at him. O'Hagan pushed her to the center of the room, and she stumbled forward.

"This is Bernadette, Mr. O'Keefe," Bill said. Bernadette continued to look down at the floor. O'Hagan gave her another shove from behind. "Give him your hand, girl," he hissed.

Bernadette drew herself up, as if steeling herself for a blow, and glanced up into Fargo's face. Her eyes were pale blue, wide, and burning with a frank and deeply felt hatred, as if she could not bear the sight of him. A slight flush crept over her pale cheeks, and her curly hair was a wild red halo around her face. She was trembling, Fargo saw, as if holding herself back. What the hell was going on here, he wondered. O'Hagan urged her forward again, and Fargo smiled encouragingly.

"Pleased to meet you, Bernadette," Fargo said, extending his hand slowly. She obviously did not want to marry him, or rather, Redmond O'Keefe.

Fargo stood waiting, his hand out. Still she hesitated. Finally, with a growl, Bill O'Hagan seized her arm and pushed it forward into Fargo's grasp. He felt her recoil at the touch of his hand.

"Don't be afraid," Fargo said to her, careful not to squeeze her small hand too tightly. If only he could tell her he was not Redmond O'Keefe, he thought. She was beautiful, delicate, but with a true determination that showed in her wide blue eyes. She withdrew her hand quickly and rubbed it on her dress. Bill O'Hagan, standing behind her, grasped her shoulders and shook her firmly.

"It's grateful you ought to be, missy, for me bringing you such a husband," he said. "There's many a girl'd be thrilled to be the wife of such a hero as Redmond O'Keefe."

Bernadette twisted in his grip.

"Leave me alone," she said quietly.

"Now, that's no way to be talking to your pa," he said. "You're being a lucky girl today. The O'Hagan blood will mix with the blood of O'Keefe, and our family will go down in Irish history as restoring the Irish Republic."

Fargo started. What the hell was O'Hagan going on about? Was it all big talk, or was he serious? He noticed suddenly that O'Hagan was watching his face closely, a question forming in his beady eyes. Fargo put a smile on his face. He'd have to remember to keep his thoughts off his face. And act like Redmond O'Keefe. But, how was that?

"I'll drink to that," Fargo said.

"Now we're talking!" responded O'Hagan. "Girl, get us that jug of poteen and put the mugs on the table. We've got some planning to be doing. Wars and weddings!"

O'Hagan slapped her on the rear as she moved off sullenly, her eyes downcast. Fargo watched as she bent to pick up her father's coat on the floor. She darted him a black look and turned away. Bill and Fargo sat down at the wide table. Bernadette brought the jug and a couple of pewter mugs and dropped them carelessly on the table.

Bill uncorked the jug and filled the mugs, sliding one across to Fargo.

"To the blessed St. Paddy . . ." O'Hagan said, raising his mug and looking expectantly at Fargo. Skye raised his and smiled broadly. Bill was waiting for an answer.

"St. Paddy," repeated Fargo and took a swig. The homemade whiskey burned the mouth and gullet as it went down. He glanced back at O'Hagan, who still sat, his mug in the air, a quizzical look on his face.

Fargo knew he had missed something. Some response to the St. Paddy toast. But what could it be? And now, O'Hagan was suspicious. Fargo thought fast.

"In the Old Country, we do it line by line now," Fargo said. "That way you get twice the drinking. Or more."

O'Hagan guffawed and took a drink.

"Well, if that be the case," he said, "then here's to the patriots of Erin too!" He raised his mug again to Fargo's and they both drank. Fargo put down his mug. The poteen was strong stuff, and he could feel it coursing through him already. He would have to be very careful to keep up his disguise as Redmond O'Keefe. It wasn't going to be easy. The best way was to get O'Hagan talking. But he'd have to be careful not to ask questions that Redmond would already know the answers to.

Fargo watched as Bill refilled their mugs to the brim. The big man had not relaxed yet, and Fargo could see the suspicion lurking behind his eyes. After they took another swig, O'Hagan put down his mug and leaned forward.

"Tell me, Mr. O'Keefe," he said, "why would it be that you don't have your brogue? You sound like an American to me."

Fargo thought fast.

"Undercover," he said. "I've been practicing this American accent since before I left Ireland. It's proved very useful."

Bill's eyes narrowed as he regarded Fargo. Skye didn't like the feel of those sharp eyes searching his face. He hardened his own gaze and stared back at O'Hagan. They sat for a long moment, staring each other down, Fargo keeping his face as hard as stone.

"But now you are being here among friends and patriots," O'Hagan said softly. "You don't need your American accent."

O'Hagan had him there, Fargo thought. For a moment he thought of faking an accent, but he didn't trust his ability to mimic an Irish brogue. Not among native speakers. Oh, hell. He thought back to the newspaper article and to all he knew about Redmond O'Keefe. What kind of man would O'Keefe be? Tough, certainly.

"I do things my own way," Fargo said, keeping his voice low and menacing. "And I don't explain. I have my reasons." He continued to stare at Bill O'Hagan. The big man shifted, then glanced down into his mug.

"For a moment there, I was beginning to doubt you," O'Hagan said, looking up again with a smile. But Fargo saw a faint shadow of suspicion still lingering in Bill's eyes. He'd won this round, but barely. O'Hagan was definitely on guard. He couldn't keep this facade up very long. The sooner he could slip away from New Dublin, the better, he thought.

"That's a fine herd of sheep I saw on my way into New Dublin," Fargo said, hoping to get O'Hagan talking.

"Aye, we've the best wool and oats this side of Galway."

"Potatoes?" Fargo asked.

"Sure, and we've got the kind don't get the disease," O'Hagan said, refilling their mugs and calling for another jug. "That would be a terrible time, the famine."

"Aye," Fargo said, shaking his head sadly and hoping the word sounded natural.

"Back in the late 40s, the O'Hagans were in the Old Country still. And starving by the dozens, like the rest of Ireland, after the potatoes failed. That's when I got the idea to come over to the new world. First, I brought over the whole clan of O'Hagans, then some O'Carrolls of Tipperary, Fitzgeralds from Cork, O'Sheas, and Doughertys. All to be coming to make a new Ireland."

"It's a great thing you've done," Fargo said, echoing the pride he heard in O'Hagan's voice.

"Aye," Bill agreed, taking another deep drink. "A great thing to be carrying on the traditions of our people. The fighting tradition. Do you know in the ancient days the first food a newborn Irish son ate was fed to him off the point of his father's sword?"

"Only fitting," Fargo said, refilling Bill's cup. "We're a fighting people." Bernadette had just entered carrying a bowl, having heard their last words. She glowered at both of them and set the bowl down with a thunk on the table, turning quickly away.

"And we're all fighting folk here in New Dublin," O'Hagan said, leaning his flushed face across the table.

"We need to be," Fargo said. This was going fairly well. All he needed to do was echo what Bill said, and it would go just fine.

"And we've been waiting for this day," Bill said. "Wanting this day to come so you can lead us. I'm as proud as I can be. But now, I'll be betting you have some questions for me."

O'Hagan looked at him expectantly. Fargo's thoughts whirled. He knew O'Hagan had something up his sleeve. Maybe an attack on the Indians? Or what? He could start there.

"I came in with the wagon train," Fargo said slowly, watching O'Hagan's face. "And we were attacked by . . ." He paused meaningfully, not sure how to frame the question and not betray his ignorance of the plot. Bernadette came into the room again with plates and spoons, setting them down on the table. Fargo noticed as she turned to go that she was trembling again, as if in fury.

"Sure and you'd be wondering if those savages would be getting in our way?" O'Hagan said. Fargo nodded and O'Hagan took the bait. "They'll be no trouble to us. We can clear out that nest of vermin later."

Fargo's head reeled. So, the mission wasn't about the Indians after all, even though O'Hagan clearly intended to battle them. But what was the objective, then?

"How many men did you get together for me?" Fargo asked, thinking of the tough men he had led in the wagon train from Denver. Bernadette carried a loaf of potato bread toward the table.

"Nearly seven hundred," O'Hagan said proudly. "But they fight like two thousand." Fargo whistled softly, despite himself.

"We'll need them," he said, hoping he sounded like he knew what he was talking about.

At his words, Bernadette dropped the loaf onto the table and the dishes clattered.

"Seven hundred souls led to their deaths!" she shouted. "And for what? All to take away land? All to bring the hatred of Ireland over here to the New World!"

O'Hagan jumped to his feet and stood swaying, his hands on the table before him to steady himself, face red.

"Shut up, girl!" he roared. "Keep your place!"

"I will not keep my place," Bernadette shouted back. "This is murder. And I won't pretend I'd be going along with it!"

O'Hagan reached out and grabbed her arm, dragging her up close to Fargo.

"You'd better be apologizing for your words," he said, giving her a shake.

"I will not," she said, stamping her foot, her face pale with fury.

"You will!" O'Hagan roared, shaking her again. Fargo winced. He felt his hands making fists and the rage welled up inside him. In another moment he was going to go at O'Hagan. With an effort of will, he held himself back. It wouldn't help himself, or Berna-

59

dette, to blow his cover now. Maybe later. Bernadette looked up at Fargo.

"You'll be having me as a wife," she said. "You'll be having my body. But you'll never be having my soul. That I swear!" She drew herself up and spit in his face, wrenching herself from O'Hagan's grip and running up the stairs.

O'Hagan took off after her with a roar. Fargo wiped his face with a napkin as he listened to the sounds of O'Hagan's angry voice from the floor above. She had a lot of strength to stand up to her father and Redmond O'Keefe. That was for certain. In another moment Bill came slowly down the stairs.

"I'd be owing you an apology, Mr. O'Keefe," said Bill.

"I can handle a woman with spirit," Fargo said, cutting him off. "Let's eat."

The two men sat down and dished out the lamb stew and potato bread. Fargo thought about what he could ask next that wouldn't betray his ignorance. He thought of Terrence O'Shaugnessey.

"Who was that mountain man who jumped me?" Fargo asked after a few moments.

"Local troublemaker," O'Hagan said with his mouth full of food. "Been here since the 30s. Been trapping. Living in the wilderness with the savages. Real Indian lover, that one. Loner. Don't trust nobody. It's time I'd be getting rid of him. Been meaning to for a long time."

"Maybe he'd be useful to us," Fargo said slowly, trying to find a way to save O'Shaugnessey's neck.

"Nay," O'Hagan said. "He's lost his love of Ireland. A man like that would be needing to be shot. Put him out of his misery. I'll do it right after we finish our eating."

Fargo took another slice of potato bread as he thought quickly.

"This O'Shaugnessey jumped *me*," Fargo said, "and

if, as you say, he's lost his love of Ireland, let me shoot him."

"Well now, Mr. O'Keefe," Bill said to him. "You being my guest, that would be only fitting." Fargo's hopes rose. He would slip away and find a way to save O'Shaugnessey. "I'll come along to watch," O'Hagan added.

Fargo felt his hopes sink. It would be hard to fake an execution with O'Hagan standing right there. But if he didn't attempt it, an innocent man would die.

Just as they were mopping up the last of the stew with the potato bread, they heard a knock at the door.

"The door's open!" O'Hagan called out. Tommy Fitzgerald put his head inside.

"Hey, boss. I've got that fellow O'Shaugnessey all locked up tight in the jailhouse," Fitzgerald said. "But he's wanting to be free something fierce. He's been shaking the bars and cursing like a sailor for most of two hours now."

"Mr. O'Keefe has asked to do the honors," O'Hagan said, pushing back from the table and rising. His voice was slurred from the poteen, Fargo noticed. "I could use a little entertainment."

"Me too, boss," said Tommy.

"Then, let's get going," Bill added, staggering toward the door.

Fargo donned his jacket with a sinking heart. There would be two of them to witness the execution of O'Shaugnessey. Maybe he and O'Shaugnessey could overpower Tommy and Bill and make a run for it. As they walked out onto the street, Fargo noticed that both men were armed. And any shots would bring out the rest of the men of New Dublin. He'd just have to wait. Watch. Hope.

They paused before a red brick building just inside the main gate and Tommy went inside. In a moment he returned, leading the handcuffed trapper by a rope.

O'Shaugnessey's eyes blazed the same hatred Fargo had seen in Bernadette's.

"Where would you be wanting to shoot him?" asked O'Hagan.

"Let's take him out in the woods beyond the town," Fargo said. "Save us the trouble of dragging out his body afterward." He might have a chance if they could get far enough away from New Dublin. In fact, he had a damn good chance beyond the walls of the town.

O'Hagan grunted assent.

"You fetch us three horses from the hackney, Tommy," he added. "Let this Indian lover take his last hike on his own two legs."

Tommy returned with Fargo's pinto, a roan, and a piebald mare. The three men mounted, Tommy holding the rope which was tied to Terrence O'Shaugnessey.

Just then, seven other men on horses came around the corner.

"Some of the men would be wanting to come along," Tommy said.

Damn, Fargo thought. Seven and two made nine. Nine men. Too many to overpower. Maybe too many to fool.

The large wooden gates swung open and they rode out onto the trail, which was muddy with the melting snow and many hoof- and footprints. Terrence walked before them.

The straw-colored sun hung low above the hills. The chinook still blew warm, and patches of earth showed through on the slopes where the snow had melted away. In the nearby field the sheep were moving in a flock toward the creek. Fargo heard their bleats and the faint tinkle of the bellwether above the sound of the steady wind.

They were just to the edge of the wood when O'Shaugnessey stumbled and faked a fall, rolling over in the snow while struggling to free himself from the rope. It held. Tommy rode up close and jerked him to his feet while the men laughed and hooted at Terrence.

"Nice try, dead man," Tommy spat at him. Terrence said nothing, but continued to walk ahead of them as they turned off the trail and entered the pine forest.

Under the boughs it was gloomy, the sun hardly penetrating the canopy of yellow pine. Underneath, what snow there was lay between the trees, undisturbed on the thick mat of pine needles. A woodpecker tapped a short distance away.

"Here," Fargo said at last. Any place in the forest was as good as any other. His success in saving O'Shaugnessey would depend on timing. And luck. He swung down from the pinto and tethered it. Now, how could he get the men away for a few moments?

"Stay on your horses," Fargo commanded. The men looked back at him questioningly. "You sure there aren't any of those Indians around? I would sure hate to risk my neck just getting rid of this scum here. If there are any, this shot will bring them down on us."

"You've got a point there," Tommy said nervously. "There's a hillock right ahead with a good view around. I could ride up and look."

"Take O'Hagan with you. He's got sharp eyes," Fargo said. "And the rest of you fan out toward the edge of the wood. Just take a quick look while I get the prisoner ready." Fargo led Terrence toward a large tree and made as if he were going to tie him up.

The men rode off obediently. As soon as they were out of earshot, Fargo wheeled toward O'Shaugnessey.

"We haven't got much time," he said in a low voice. The trapper looked back at him, startled by the change in his tone. "I'm not O'Keefe. And I'm going to try to get you out of this alive. But you'll have to play along with me." While he spoke, Fargo reloaded his Colt.

"I'm going to shoot just beside you, real fast, six times. With luck, the shots will go into the woods behind you and in the dark, they won't notice. When I shoot, you jump and grab your belly. Fall forward. That way they might not see you're not bleeding. Your body'd better jump every time you hear a gun go off or you're a dead man."

"Why are you doing this for me?" O'Shaugnessey asked.

"Let's just say I don't like the smell of New Dublin," Fargo said. He opened his mouth to say more, but saw several of the men returning. "I'll teach you, you yellowbelly," Fargo shouted at O'Shaugnessey. "You'll stand up to this like a man! No blindfold!"

They were drawing nearer, and in another moment Fargo spotted O'Hagan heading back. It was almost completely dark under the trees. Suddenly Fargo backed away from O'Shaugnessey and drew his Colt and stood cocking the hammer over and over.

"Let's all shoot at him," one of the men shouted from his horse. "See who gets him between the eyes first." Fargo saw O'Shaugnessey's gaze dart toward the men. But he didn't flinch.

"He's mine," Fargo said in a low voice.

"That's right," Bill shouted as he rode up. He uncorked a bottle he had brought along with him. "I promised him to O'Keefe."

He'd have to make this good, Fargo realized, or they'd never believe it. If the men suspected something wasn't right, they'd draw and shoot.

In an instant Fargo raised his Colt and aimed just over O'Shaugnessey's shoulder into the dark woods beyond. Hell, he hoped the bullet wouldn't strike a rock and ricochet. For a moment he looked down the length of the barrel into the dark eyes of Terrence O'Shaugnessey. Doubt flickered for a moment in Terrence's face, and Fargo wondered what he must be feeling. O'Shaugnessey would be wondering if Fargo had lied and if this wasn't some cruel joke played on a condemned man.

"Any last words, O'Shaugnessey?" Fargo called out.

"Rot in hell!" he shouted back.

Fargo squeezed the trigger and the Colt exploded. O'Shaugnessey recoiled, a little later than he might have if he'd been shot, but it was pretty convincing, Fargo thought. The shot zinged past Terrence. It must have struck a tree or the earth beyond. He squeezed the trigger again, quickly four more times in quick succession as Terrence slumped forward onto the ground and jerked at each retort. The men shouted and laughed. Skye lifted the barrel of the gun slowly before him and blew the smoke away.

"Let's get out of here," Fargo said, turning back. O'Hagan had drawn his pistol and was waving it.

"This one's for St. Paddy!" O'Hagan shouted, taking another long pull from his bottle and taking an unsteady aim at O'Shaugnessey's body. Fargo thought fast.

"Over there!" Fargo shouted. "Indians! Coming down the hill!" He aimed the Colt up the hill and fired his last bullet into the empty woods. Several of the men drew their guns and began blasting away in the same direction. "Get out of here! Ride for your lives!"

In the darkening woods, the men panicked and began to retreat, but O'Hagan still aimed at O'Shaugnessey, the barrel wavering.

"Let's get out of here!" Fargo shouted again to distract him. O'Hagan fired. Fargo saw O'Shaugnessey's body twitch again in the near darkness as O'Hagan wheeled about on his horse and followed the rest of his men. Fargo leapt onto the pinto and followed through the woods, bringing up the rear.

Sonofabitch, he thought to himself. It had all happened so fast. There was no way to tell if O'Hagan had hit Terrence or not. As he followed the men through the darkness of the pine forest, he realized he could easily get away from them and go back to check up on O'Shaugnessey. Then he could ride away. Leave New Dublin behind forever. The thought came and went. He continued to ride behind the men.

He was going back to New Dublin, Fargo realized. There was something very wrong there. And the only ones who could see it were him and Bernadette. And O'Shaugnessey, who might now be dead. He thought of Bernadette, of her frank blue eyes. Nothing like unfinished business, he thought. He couldn't run away. Not now. Not ever.

4

"Good thing you spotted those Indians sneaking up on us, Redmond," O'Hagan said as they reined in before his house. "Let's celebrate O'Shaugnessey's demise with a wee drop." O'Hagan dismounted ponderously, along with the other men. Dusk had given way to night during the ride back, and now the golden lights of the village winked in the darkness. Fargo slid down from the pinto. Seamus O'Carroll approached to take the reins.

"I'll take care of my own horse," Fargo said. "Then I'll come in." He needed some time to plan his next move. O'Hagan grunted and shrugged as Fargo moved off.

O'Carroll and Fargo entered the dark stables, the warm smell of hay and horse hung in the air. O'Carroll lit a lamp and began leading the rest of the mounts into the shelter. Fargo selected a wide stall and led in the Ovaro.

Fargo stroked the black and white pinto absentmindedly as he thought over the day's events. The one thing he did not want was another protracted conversation with Bill O'Hagan. It wouldn't be long before O'Hagan realized that he was not Redmond O'Keefe. Fargo leaned down and tapped the fetlock of the pinto. It raised its hoof for his inspection, and Fargo pried loose a small stone. He checked the other hooves and then gave it a quick rubdown with a body brush. Was O'Shaugnessey still alive? Had O'Hagan hit him with that final potshot in the darkness of the wood? Or had Terrence, obeying Fargo's instructions, jumped at the report of O'Hagan's gun too? Fargo swore silently. There was every chance Terrence's body was stone cold under that tree in the woods.

He poured some oats into the trough along with a mound of timothy hay. And then there was Bernadette. He thought about O'Hagan's treatment of her. She was being forced to marry Redmond O'Keefe against her will. And she knew what was going on in the town. He was sure of that. If he could only convince her that he was not Redmond, she might tell him what was going on. But how to get to talk to her alone? The pinto was munching happily on the oats as Fargo left the stable.

Fargo paused outside Bill O'Hagan's house. There were three upstairs windows, one of them lit. Probably Bernadette's, he thought. The rough stone exterior of the house would be easy to scale. He could be up there in an instant, he thought, glancing up and down the street. There was no one in sight. Moving quickly, Fargo crossed to the house and began to haul himself up, finding finger- and toe-holds in the rough stone.

He was almost to the window when he heard the sound of approaching hooves. Fargo froze, clinging to the side of the stone house, a good ten feet above the ground. He held his breath as the rider neared, hoping he wouldn't stop or notice the odd sight of a man climbing up the side of O'Hagan's house. The horse kept going and the sound diminished. Fargo breathed again. He had to get in the window soon or risk discovery. He climbed up another foot until he grasped the windowsill and gradually eased his head upward to look inside.

The room was cozy and warm with quilts and rugs. A small fire burned in a stone fireplace. A bed was piled with thick feather comforters and pillows. There was no one there. Fargo tugged at the casement. The window wasn't locked and swung open. He eased his head and shoulders inside the window. Just then he heard voices—two women—coming nearer, and he struggled to get himself into the room. The door opened.

Bernadette whirled into the room, but didn't notice him half inside the window.

"I don't want to be hearing any of your ugly talk!" she shouted, turning back toward the door and trying to hold it shut.

"You just don't want to be hearing the truth!" the other voice screamed. Fargo recognized the voice as Maureen's as he pulled his legs inside the window. The door pushed half open as Bernadette fought to keep it closed. Fargo sighted a folding screen in one corner and ducked behind it just as the door flew open, throwing Bernadette down onto the floor.

"That'll teach you to try to be keeping me out of your room," Maureen said. Fargo knelt behind the folding wooden screen. He pushed aside some lacy garments which were tossed over the screen and peered through the crack between the panels. Maureen stood in the doorway of Bernadette's room, her black brows lowered, her hands on her hips. Bernadette rolled to her feet and got up, brushing herself off.

"Just leave me alone, Maureen," she said tiredly, pulling her wavy red hair back from her face. "That's all I'd be asking. I'm tired of fighting. I hate fighting."

"What kind of Irish are you to be tired of fighting?" Maureen said, coming into the room and shutting the door behind her. "The only thing in the world worth having are things worth fighting for."

"Not that kind of fighting," Bernadette said. "It's the unnecessary fighting I'm opposed to. I don't want to fight with you."

"But you want to fight our father." Maureen paced back and forth across the rag rug.

"Yes," Bernadette said slowly, seating herself on the bed.

"Because you'd not be wanting to obey him."

"I don't want to marry a man I don't love," Bernadette said quickly. Fargo saw Bernadette's pale face flush. "And I . . . I don't love Redmond O'Keefe. At least not yet. I don't even like what he stands for."

"You should be happy to do whatever our father tells you to," Maureen said. "Even marrying a man you don't love."

"Then why don't you marry Tommy Fitzgerald?" Bernadette spat back. "Father would like for you to marry his deputy. Why don't you do that? Because Tommy's not good enough for you?"

"Shut up!" Maureen shouted, standing stock still in the center of the rug. Fargo saw her dark eyes glitter and her brows lower. She looked entirely different from the warm and willing woman he had held in his arms the night before. "I'm tired of you getting the best of everything. You get Redmond O'Keefe, hero of all of Ireland, and what did I get?" Maureen's voice rose hysterically. "First I got O'Shea, the town drunk. Now I got Tommy, the town fool. I'm tired of getting second best."

Maureen sank into a rocking chair and hid her face in her hands. Bernadette jumped to her feet and rushed over to kneel beside her.

"I'm sorry, Maureen," she said, putting her arm around her sister. "That wasn't fair of me. I know it's been hard on you. Look, let's be friends."

Maureen was strangely silent. Not sobbing. Not speaking. Finally, she looked up at Bernadette.

"All right," she said. "We'll be friends." Bernadette gave her a hug, and Fargo could see a smile on Maureen's face as she held her sister. "So, tell me," Maureen said, drawing back from Bernadette's embrace. "What do you think of your intended, Mr. O'Keefe?"

Bernadette rose to her feet and returned to sit on the bed.

"Well," she said slowly, "I don't like his fighting ways, but he is very handsome."

"His pictures were handsome," Maureen said, encouragingly. "Did you think he was as handsome in person?" Fargo didn't like her tone of voice, nor the fact that she wasn't telling Bernadette that they had met already. How much would she tell her sister anyway?

"What surprised me were his eyes," said Bernadette, in a faraway voice as if reliving their meeting. "His eyes were very kind. And he seemed to be sensible. Not at all the kind of man I was expecting."

"He's a great hero," Maureen said. "Strong, forceful, courageous . . ."

"Yes," Bernadette agreed. "I could see all that in him, but there was something else too. A kind of understanding. A gentleness. Maybe . . ." There was a long silence and Fargo saw Bernadette's face take on a dreamy look.

"Maybe what?" Maureen said, her voice honeysweet.

"Maybe I could learn to love Redmond O'Keefe," Bernadette said quietly. "Maybe, if he loved me too, I could teach him about this country. About how we don't need more hate and warfare here. How we don't need more fighting."

"But he's a patriot," Maureen said, her voice growing cold. "Fighting is his religion."

"That may be," Bernadette said. "But, there was something about him that made me feel he would be a friend to me, as well as a husband. I could trust him."

"Really?" Maureen said, her voice cutting like ice. "And how do you think he will be in bed?"

71

"Maureen!" Bernadette blushed and looked away.

"I'll tell you how he'll be in bed," Maureen said, rising to her feet and walking over to stand above her sister.

"You have more experience than I have in those matters," Bernadette said quickly. "But I guess I'll find out eventually." It was clear she was eager to change the subject.

"Why don't I just tell you?" Maureen said.

"Stop teasing me."

"He's great in bed," Maureen said. "The best I've ever had."

"What are you talking about?"

"I know because he spent last night with me," Maureen said. Bernadette looked up at her sister, her face pale.

"You're lying."

"Ask Tommy. Tommy brought him to my house. And ask Redmond what we did all night. Would you like to hear all the details?" Maureen laughed into Bernadette's shocked face. "You see, this time I got the best. And when I tell father what happened, he'll force Redmond to marry me. Redmond doesn't want you anyway. He wants a real woman like me."

"Get out!" Bernadette said, her voice low with fury. She stood and with a sudden burst of energy pushed her sister out the door, locking it behind her. Fargo heard Maureen's laughter as she walked down the hall. "Bitch!" Bernadette said to the closed door.

Fargo watched for a few minutes as Bernadette paced up and down. He thought about coming forward and explaining. But what could he say? Now that she knew he had slept with Maureen she mistrusted him completely. Would she believe that he wasn't Redmond O'Keefe? How could he prove it to her?

Fargo had just made up his mind to step forward when Bernadette suddenly stopped pacing and began

72

to unbutton her blouse. In a moment she had slipped out of it, leaving her in her lacy camisole which barely covered her small high breasts. She swiftly unbuttoned her skirt and petticoats, letting them drop, exposing her slim hips and long legs in bloomers. If he stepped forward now, he realized, she would be extremely embarrassed. He could only hope she wouldn't discover him and he could slip away.

Bernadette turned toward the screen and lifted the camisole off over her head, freeing her creamy breasts with their delicate pink tips. She stripped off her bloomers and Fargo saw her white garters, long slim stocking-clad legs, and the auburn tangle of nap between her legs. She balanced one foot and then the other on the bed as she undid her garters and rolled down her stockings. Then she straightened up, completely naked. Fargo saw her suddenly shiver.

"Now, how did I leave that window open?" she muttered aloud as she walked across the room toward the window.

Fargo shrank back into the corner behind the screen, realizing that as she neared the window she would spot him. He tried to inch over the screen so that it would be between him and the window. He couldn't move it fast enough without attracting her attention or making a noise. He watched as she slammed the casement closed and pivoted toward him. Her eyes widened as she caught his gaze and her mouth dropped open.

She screamed with fright and, suddenly realizing she was naked, covered herself with her hands as she ran toward the bed.

Fargo stepped out, holding his hands in front of him trying to shush her.

"Bernadette! Quiet! I need to talk to you!"

"Get out of my room!" Bernadette shouted, pulling a quilt off the bed to wrap around her. "How dare you!"

"I need to talk to you! I'm not Redmond O'Keefe!"

"Well you're not a gentleman! A gentleman would look away!"

"That's not a gentleman. That's a damn fool," he said, enjoying the sight of her. "But in any case, I'm not Redmond O'Keefe." Bernadette was suddenly silent, puzzlement written on her face. Fargo heard voices below and the sound of feet on the stairs. Damn, he thought. No escape.

"Look," he said, his voice low. "I'm not Redmond. I can help you. But I need some information."

"What's this screaming like a banshee? What's going on in there, Bernadette?" O'Hagan shouted from the other side of the door. The doorknob jiggled as he tried it. The door was locked. Bernadette looked wildly from Fargo to the door and back, not knowing what to do. "Bernadette?" he called again.

Her mouth opened, not knowing what to answer. Fargo backed away, one finger to his lips, intending to hide again behind the screen. Just then, a violent thud hit the door, and the lock gave way. The door flew open, and Bill O'Hagan stood in the doorway. His face broke into a wide smile as he saw Fargo standing there. He glanced at Bernadette who cowered by the bed, covering her nakedness with the quilt.

Bill O'Hagan guffawed.

"Well, Saints alive!" he muttered. "Mr. O'Keefe has come acourting in his own way. Come along with you, Mr. O'Keefe. That'll have to wait for your wedding day, 'less she be awilling."

Fargo shrugged and shot a look at Bernadette. She was watching him closely, curiosity on her face. He could almost read her thoughts. If you're not Redmond O'Keefe, she seemed to be thinking, then who are you? He'd find another opportunity to talk to Bernadette alone, he decided. The next time she'd be willing to hear him out.

"Can't blame a man for wanting to jump the gun," Fargo said to O'Hagan as they walked out of the room. O'Hagan chuckled. Behind his back Fargo gestured to Bernadette, a kind of wave with the fingers crossed. He hoped she'd read his signal as he intended it: don't believe what you hear me say—trust your feelings about me—I'm not Redmond O'Keefe.

O'Hagan and Fargo descended the stair. Tommy Fitzgerald, Seamus O'Carroll, and the rest of the men lounged around the long wooden table. Maureen and several other women scurried back and forth with pitchers and bottles and glasses. Maureen looked up, surprised to see Fargo coming downstairs.

"Look at the eager bridegroom I'd be finding upstairs in Bernadette's room!" O'Hagan announced. The men at the table laughed and toasted Fargo. Maureen's face registered shock, then a flash of anger, before she turned away.

"Just wanted to see what I was getting into," Fargo said. He tried to inflect a little Irish brogue into his voice. It wasn't hard, but he didn't want to overdo it.

"Well, you'll not be getting into it tonight. Aye, you'd be sounding more and more like the Redmond O'Keefe we've all been expecting," Bill said, slapping him hard on the back. "Let's have another round, and you tell us about all the doings in the Old Country."

Fargo swore silently to himself as he kept a smile on his face. He looked at the circle of expectant faces around the table. It was one thing to fool O'Hagan for a few minutes, but this looked like an all-night drinking bout with a dozen men, who might all have a dozen questions for him. None of which he knew the answers to. What kind of man would Redmond be, Fargo asked himself again. Impatient, he decided.

"I don't have time to tell tales of Ireland," Fargo said. "I need to know how we're going to go about doing what we need to do here." There was a silence as the men looked back at him. They shifted uncomfortably. O'Hagan nodded thoughtfully.

"Want to get right down to business, do you?" he said. "That's disappointing. And it's not our way here in New Dublin. We need to have some tales. Some drink. Some singing. Then, and only then, can we can get down to business."

"Some singing!" one of the men muttered, his voice slurred.

"We'll get Maureen to give us a song," O'Hagan said. "That'll loosen up our hearts and our tongues. Maureen!"

Maureen appeared, having heard her father's words, carrying a small harp. The women refilled the mugs with whiskey as Maureen plucked the strings. She missed a few of the notes, but Fargo recognized the familiar tune. He knew it as a love song and was surprised when she began to sing it in a strong, clear voice with a kind of quiet anger, to different words:

"Come, you patriots of Ireland,
Hope's shining bright 'midst our pain.
For River Shannon's flowing wild and free,
Crushing our oats, milling our grain.
  Oh, it's brave they will be,
  All the true Shamrock men,
  And there'll be blood in the bread
  Of our dear Ireland.
Add your tears to the waters now,
We'll crush our foes like grain,
And we'll never stop fighting
Till Ireland is Irish once again.
  Oh, it's brave they will be,
  All the true Shamrock men,
  And there'll be blood in the bread
  Of our dear Ireland."

The men joined in on the chorus and Fargo mimed along, as if he knew the words, singing out the second time around when he had learned the lyrics. Finally the song ended and the men applauded as Maureen bowed and left the room.

"Now we're in the spirit," O'Hagan said, taking another draught of whiskey and smacking his lips. "Tell us, Mr. O'Keefe, what would be the thinking of our confederates? And what about our Fenian brothers in New York? Proud they must be of our plans to free the country."

The men leaned forward, eager to hear what he had to say. Fargo hesitated.

"Sure, they're proud," he said. "New Dublin is a town to be proud of." The men smiled at one another, shaking their heads.

"But what of the politics back home?" O'Hagan pressed. "We've all been wanting to hear from you who will win the next elections? Will they be one of us?"

Fargo searched his mind for anything he knew about Irish politics. He just didn't know enough about Ireland to fake it much longer.

"No one can tell," Fargo said with a noncommittal shrug. "We can only hope for the best." Outwardly the answer seemed to satisfy O'Hagan.

"I thought as much," Bill said, nodding and resting back in his chair. But Fargo saw that in his eyes, half hidden by the heavy puffiness of his face, the faint glimmer of suspicion had returned.

"Tell us the news, man," Seamus O'Carroll said insistently, leaning forward. "Tell us how it is to be home. God I miss Ireland. Graven in my soul are the red bogs and the mists rising off the loughs."

"Aye," said another. "We O'Neills left our bones up in the north, around our old castle, Grianan of Aileach. It was two hundred years and more, but there's a part of me'll always be buried there alongside them. Damn the English and the Protestants!" He thumped his mug down on the table, sloshing the poteen. "Let their blood water our dry graves for taking away our land!"

"Aye," said several of the others. The men were totally drunk, several of them slumping forward on the table.

"Now, let's not be giving in to despair," O'Hagan cut in. Despite the alcohol Bill had consumed, he seemed to be in full possession of his senses. "Not in front of our distinguished guest." Fargo heard the sly menace in O'Hagan's voice, and he thought of Maureen's voice as she tried to lure her sister into admitting her attraction to Redmond. What trap would O'Hagan set for him? And how could he slip away? "Tell me straight, Mr. O'Keefe. What do they think, back in Ireland, of our invasion plans? Are they pleased? And do you think we can bargain successfully with them afterward?"

Fargo's thoughts whirled. Invasion plans? Invading where? And what bargain? After what? He became aware that O'Hagan was looking at him carefully, and the other men were watching. Fargo felt the sweat trickle down his back. He took a long drink to cover his silence. His answer would have to sound authentic, he thought. But he must not say too much.

"They are impressed with the invasion plans," Fargo said, nodding. "Very impressed. They think we will be successful." O'Hagan continued to watch him silently, expectantly. Fargo remembered a map of Ireland he had seen once with the major cities drawn on it. He had a flash of inspiration. "When we succeed, the name of New Dublin, and all of our names, will be famous from south to north, from Cork to Londonderry!" he said, raising his mug high.

Instantly, the room erupted in shouts and motion, the men jumping to their feet and backing away from the table, several of them drawing their guns and pointing them at Fargo. Only O'Hagan remained at the table opposite Fargo. Fargo lowered his mug slowly to the table, keeping his face placid. What had he said?

"What was that, Mr. O'Keefe?" asked O'Hagan. "I think none of us heard you right."

"I heard him right, boss," Tommy Fitzgerald cut in. "I heard him say Londonderry."

"A slip of the tongue," Fargo said trying to look unconcerned and taking a swig. What the hell was wrong with Londonderry?

"Not a slip of the tongue any true Irishman would make," O'Hagan said, his eyes narrowing. Fargo did not like his gaze. And the men had not relaxed yet. They stood about the table, whispering among themselves, uneasy. "No true Irishman has called Derry by that name since they took it from us and slaughtered our people. Londonderry!" he spat. "That name burns my tongue!"

"Mine too," Fargo said quietly, thinking fast. "But I've trained myself to say it, since I've been traveling undercover."

O'Hagan's bushy eyebrows raised as he regarded Fargo. The men mumbled, and several of them sat back down. But the suspicious glint didn't leave Bill's eyes.

"I don't like it," Bill said at last. "There'd be many a thing aren't adding up about you, Mr. O'Keefe. Patriot or not. I don't like your accent. And I don't like your explanation."

It was about to get ugly, Fargo decided. He calculated his chances as his muscles tensed, and he became acutely aware of the heavy Colt in his holster. A dozen men. Armed. Drunk. But not drunk enough. No chance, he thought. He'd have to wait and see. Try to talk his way out.

"Take him," O'Hagan said suddenly. Fargo drew in a flash, but three men jumped him instantly and he realized that shooting one or two of them would only make matters worse.

"Hold on," Fargo said, keeping his voice good-natured. "You've got to be kidding."

"Take his gun. Lock him up for the night," O'Hagan said. "Tomorrow I'll get to the bottom of this."

"You're making a big mistake," Fargo said as Tommy Fitzgerald took his pistol. If he didn't put up too much of a struggle, he thought, they might not search him and find the throwing knife strapped to his ankle.

Fitzgerald led as five of the men escorted Fargo out to the street. They were wary, and there was no chance to distract them or slip away on the short walk to the jailhouse. Tommy led the way inside the small stone building, lit an oil lamp, and took a key down from a nail on the wall, using it to unlock the town's one jail cell.

"In you go, Mr. O'Keefe, until you get your Irish tongue back again." He slammed the barred door and locked it, hanging the key again on the nail on the opposite wall. He stowed Fargo's Colt in the desk drawer and blew out the lamp. The men left. Fargo heard their boots crunching in the snow, ice-crusted in the night cold, and then it was silent.

The cell was spacious and empty, save a narrow rope bed with a folded blanket and a bucket standing in one corner. Ah, the hospitality of New Dublin, Fargo thought, contrasting it to the cozy night before he had spent with Maureen. That bitch, he thought, anger welling in him as he thought of her using him— or Redmond—to taunt Bernadette.

But, he thought, his big problem now was Bill O'Hagan. Morning would come soon. And O'Hagan's suspicions were full-blown. He wouldn't be able to get away with pretending to be Redmond O'Keefe at their next meeting.

Fargo began to examine the cell inch by inch. He

stood on the bed and tugged at the bars on the window. They were deeply embedded into the stone sill of the window. Only one of them was loose and that one only very slightly. Even if he could work it free from the stone sill—and it would probably take the rest of the night—the bars were set so close together that he would have to remove two of them in order to slide out.

He hopped down and tried the bars in the front of the cell. All firm. He pressed against the lock of the cell door. It was a heavy one, well built. Not one to be easily forced. Damn, he thought. He reached down and slid the throwing knife out of its ankle sheath. Using the point, he slipped it between the door and the iron doorjamb until he felt the resistance of the catch. For the next half hour he tried to jimmy the bolt. But it was too heavy to give and he didn't want to risk snapping the knife blade. Then he tried picking the lock, but the knife point wasn't narrow enough to catch the levers and lift the tumblers. Realizing it was useless, he put the knife away and turned his attention to the room outside the cell. He peered into the darkness and saw a small potbellied stove, which gave off a vague warmth and a faint red glow. The embers were almost out. It would be a cold night, Fargo thought. A wooden desk stood on the opposite wall, and a subtle glint showed him where the key to the cell hung on the nail. It was a long way across the room.

Skye looked at the cot again. Rope. Pieces of wood. He took the cot apart in his mind, stretched out the short planks end to end, binding them with rope and his clothing. Still wouldn't reach across the room to the key. He gave up on that idea.

Fargo sighed with resignation and turned toward the bed. Nothing to do but wait. And get some sleep. Tomorrow promised to be an interesting day. Maybe his last. He stretched out on the rickety bed, which creaked under him, and pulled up the thin blanket. The cold air drifted in through the barred window. Something tickled his cheek and he slapped it. Fleas. Great, he thought, wishing he were anywhere in the world but in New Dublin.

Fargo opened his eyes as he heard footsteps approaching. The sun was up and a chill was in the air. He sat up and swung his feet over the edge of the cot, as Tommy Fitzgerald and two other men entered.

"Have a good night's rest, Mr. O'Keefe?" Fitzgerald asked pleasantly.

"I can't say much for American hospitality," said Fargo.

"Mr. O'Hagan sent his apologies for last night," said Fitzgerald.

"He's finally come to his senses, and he's letting me out of here?"

"Not exactly," Fitzgerald answered. "I'm sure you understand that Mr. O'Hagan can't be too careful. A man in his position stays alive by staying cautious. He's wanting to talk to you as soon as possible to straighten this thing out. But he had to be going to check on business," Fitzgerald said. "He'll be back to New Dublin tomorrow morning. Meanwhile, we brought you some breakfast. Mr. O'Hagan wanted you to be as comfortable as possible, under the circumstances."

Fargo realized that O'Hagan had probably begun to worry that he might have made a mistake by locking up O'Keefe. If he had jailed the famous Irish patriot without due cause, there could be trouble from O'Keefe's supporters. That's why he was getting an apology and breakfast this morning, Fargo decided.

Still, they weren't taking any chances. The men drew their guns and motioned for Fargo to stand away from the cell door as Fitzgerald hooked the key and unlocked it. They watched carefully as a pail of fresh water and a basket was put inside. They locked the door again, checking it twice, and one of the men lit a fire in the stove. The two men left, and Fitzgerald remained behind reading the newspaper, his feet propped up on the desk.

Fargo washed up, using the cloth from the breakfast basket to dry himself. The stove quickly warmed the room. In the basket he found a tin pot of hot coffee, a cup, and soda biscuits with slices of beef. He seated himself on the cot and in a few moments felt much better.

The day passed slowly. Fargo tried to engage Fitzgerald in conversation, but the man simply continued to read his newspaper. Nevertheless, Fargo had the distinct impression that Fitzgerald was eyeing him continually when his back was turned.

For an hour Fargo paced back and forth in the cell, stretching his legs. He climbed up onto the cot and looked out at New Dublin. The main street storefronts framed the half-frozen waterfall with the waterwheel relentlessly turning. Townspeople went back and forth quickly like ants. Once he caught the strain of a familiar tune and heard the words ". . . there'll be blood in the bread of our dear Ireland," and in another moment, the fur-bundled figure of Maureen hurried past, singing absentmindedly. He continued to watch for some time and then spotted the small, dapper shape of the photographer Oscar Wyndham, his bald head gleaming in the morning sun.

As Fargo's eyes swept the view, he caught a slight movement up high on the cliff at the top of the falls overlooking New Dublin. He continued to look at the spot. There it was again in the tangle of branches at the top of the waterfall. Bigger than a bird. Maybe an animal, he thought. But no animal would stand at the top of a cliff overlooking a human settlement. Blackfoot? Scouting out the town for an attack? If so, an Indian attack would be really interesting from inside a jail cell, he decided. He continued to watch, but saw no more movement. When he tired of looking out the window, Fargo climbed down. There was more coffee in the pot, but it was cold now. That gave him an idea. If he could only lure Fitzgerald near enough.

"Hey, Tommy," Fargo called. "Could you put this coffee on that stove for me. It's just too cold to drink."

Fitzgerald sighed and rose, folding his paper. He ambled toward the bars, but then stopped some distance away. He looked at Fargo, his eyes, so close together, narrowing.

"Mr. O'Hagan's been telling me to be more than a little careful around you," he said. "Why don't you just reach that coffeepot between the bars and set it out here on the floor? Then go stand by the wall."

Fargo cursed inwardly. Well, that wasn't going to work. Of course he had the throwing knife. He could kill Fitzgerald. But what would be the point? It wouldn't get him free. Well, at least he'd get a hot cup of coffee.

Lunch came with the same careful routine. After lunch three men came, and they handcuffed him and led him out to the street so that he could walk up and down for half an hour. As he paced back and forth, he glanced up at the cliff and saw the faint movement again. No mistaking it this time. Indian? Or somebody else? He watched until he could see nothing more. Then he spent the afternoon napping in the cell.

By dusk Fitzgerald was restless. He stood and stretched several times, building up the fire and poking it, lighting the oil lamp and fiddling with the burning wick. The oil was getting low. He sat down with the same paper he'd been reading all day. Fargo wondered if he was memorizing it or if he was just a damn slow reader. The lamp finally flickered and smoked. The lamp was out of oil and the flame died. Fitzgerald stood up in the gloom.

"Your supper will be along soon," Fitzgerald said. "I'll check up on you in the morning."

When Fitzgerald left, Fargo glanced about the cell again, hoping he'd missed some chance for escape. Nothing. Then he heard the sound of footsteps approaching . . . a man alone, pausing at the door of the jailhouse. Fargo's hopes rose. The door opened slowly, and the smell of warm stew filled Fargo's nostrils. He felt a rush of happiness, but not because of the food. The man, his black felt hat pulled down low over his face, was alone. This was his chance for escape. Fargo bent down in the near darkness and slid the knife out of the sheath.

The man quickly shut the door behind him and glanced around the darkened room once, then crossed to the desk and set the dinner basket down. He hurriedly reached up and removed the key ring from the wall. Fargo's head spun as the man walked toward the cell door. This was too easy. The man would unlock the door, go all the way back to the desk to get the dinner basket, leaving the door open and his back turned?

Fargo tensed his muscles to spring, as the man eased the key into the lock and turned it with a rusty squeal. The door opened.

"Let's get out of here," the man said quietly. The voice was Terrence O'Shaugnessey's.

5

"Terrence O'Shaugnessey!" Fargo said. "So Bill O'Hagan's potshot didn't get you after all."

"Too much poteen, I reckon," Terrence said.

"No doubt," Fargo said. "How'd you find me?"

"I spent the day watching the town."

"From on top of the cliff?" Fargo asked.

"You've got sharp eyes," said Terrence. "I saw them leading you around outside in the afternoon. I thought they might catch on to you eventually. I don't even know who you are, but you saved my life and I figure I owe you one. So I slipped down the cliff on foot. I spotted two fellows carrying your dinner and gave them each a good crack on the head. They won't come around until morning."

"Glad you came. Let's talk more later. We've got to hurry."

Fargo crossed quickly to the desk and removed his Colt from the drawer. He saw paper, ink, and a quill pen and had a sudden thought. The role of Redmond O'Keefe might still prove useful to him, he realized. He wanted to keep Bill O'Hagan guessing about his true identity.

He dipped the pen, and squinting in the dark, he wrote in large letters: "Bill O'Hagan—Thanks for the hospitality. You should know by now that no cage can hold Redmond O'Keefe. I'll be back to finish our business."

Fargo placed the note on the cot and relocked the

cell, replacing the key on the nail. That would keep them guessing. Terrence waited at the door, held it open a crack, and peered out to watch the street.

They slipped out of the jailhouse and edged along the street, ducking into doorways when any of the townspeople walked by. Fargo signaled as they passed the stable, and they entered. It was silent except for the quiet rustle of the horses. Fargo saddled the Ovaro, and Terrence selected a bay, and they led the horses out into the street. As they neared the front gate, Terrence stopped short.

"Oh, hell," he muttered. "We've missed it."

"Missed what?" Fargo asked.

Terrence pointed ahead. The large wooden gate was bolted shut, and four men—two on the ground and two on the parapet above—stood guard.

"The main gate shuts every night at seven o'clock," he said. "To get out of town after hours, we need a pass from Bill O'Hagan."

"Is there any other way out?" Fargo asked.

"Up the cliff," said Terrence. "Not an easy climb."

And they couldn't bring the horses, Fargo realized. They needed their mounts. Without them, they wouldn't get very far.

"We'll have to hole up for the night somewhere in New Dublin," said Fargo. He thought of the little photographer.

"Come on," he said. They turned their horses around and Fargo led them toward the storefront marked OSCAR WYNDHAM PHOTOGRAPH GALLERY. The front windows were dark, but a light around the back of the building drew his attention. Oscar probably lived behind his store. They led the horses down the side alley and found a small shed off a closed yard in the back of the building. They tethered the horses inside the shed. Fargo and Terrence climbed the short stair, and Fargo rapped on the warped wooden door.

"Who's there?" Oscar's voice called from inside.

Footsteps approached and paused just on the other side of the door. "Who is it?"

"We need some help," Fargo said quietly in case anyone was wandering nearby.

"What kind of help?" Oscar asked, not opening the door. "Who is it anyway?"

"I came in your shop yesterday," Fargo said. "You remember me. I'm not Redmond O'Keefe."

They heard a breathless gasp from the other side of the door.

"Bill O'Hagan put you in jail!"

"He did, but I'm out now," Fargo said. He glanced at Terrence who raised his eyebrows. Oscar did not sound like he was going to be immediately helpful.

"But . . . but . . . why did you come here?" said Oscar. "I can't get mixed up in this."

Fargo realized that every minute's delay increased the risk of discovery. Oscar clearly needed a little encouragement.

"Listen, Oscar," Fargo said, winking at Terrence, "I know exactly where you're standing behind this door. I have my Colt trained right at your belly. Move one muscle and I'll pull the trigger."

"What . . . what do you want from me?" Oscar's voice quivered.

"Unlock the door, Oscar," Fargo said.

They heard the sound of fumbling at the latch, and the door swung open. Oscar's eyes were round and scared. He glanced at Fargo, registering surprise not to see a gun in his hand. Fargo and Terrence pushed inside, shutting and locking the door behind them.

"Thanks, Oscar," Fargo said. "We really appreciate your willing help."

Oscar's mouth opened and shut silently several times while Terrence checked out the other rooms to make sure no one else was there. Fargo shut the curtains at the windows, and he and Terrence took seats at the kitchen table.

"You're . . . you're Terrence O'Shaugnessey!" Oscar said finally. "I've heard about you. You're the wild man who lives with the Indians."

Oscar's fear couldn't quite disguise the note of admiration in his voice. Terrence nodded at him. Oscar drew his short frame up to his full height, and he seemed to lose his apprehension for a moment.

"So now, what can I do for you, Mr. Terrence O'Shaugnessey and Mr. Skye Fargo-not-O'Keefe?" Oscar asked.

Now it was Terrence's turn to look surprised.

"Skye Fargo?" he repeated, turning toward him. "So that's who you are. I've always wanted to run into you. But not under these circumstances." Fargo nodded and smiled at the trapper.

"You sure look a helluva lot like Redmond O'Keefe," Terrence said, shaking his head in disbelief. "At least like the picture I saw of him."

"Just my luck," said Fargo. "And I figure as long as I stumbled into O'Keefe's affairs, I'd better find out what the hell he's up to."

"But since you're not Redmond O'Keefe," Oscar said slowly, "then what happens when the real O'Keefe shows up?"

"He'll be in for a big surprise." Fargo said. "Now, let's get down to business. I'll take some coffee, Oscar. Food if you've got it. And I want to hear everything both of you know about New Dublin, Redmond O'Keefe, Bill O'Hagan, and what he's got up his sleeve."

For an hour Fargo listened. Terrence told how he had come from Ireland to trap in what was then unorganized territory and how he had made friends with the Blackfoot Indians. Oscar listened, his eyes growing wide. Then Terrence told how he watched as settlers began to arrive. The town of New Dublin had been a planned village run by Bill O'Hagan from the very start.

"It's bad enough that the New Dubliners pushed the Blackfoot out of this area," O'Shaugnessey said. "The tribes are not real happy about that. But now O'Hagan is bringing in these wagon trains of hired guns."

"That made me suspicious too!" cut in Oscar, thumping his fist on the table, eager to be part of the conversation.

"I came into town with some of them," said Fargo. "They're tough guys. But they're not being billeted in New Dublin."

"No," Terrence said. "O'Hagan's set up a camp over by the Sage River. I've seen it. Looks like a regular army camp with a hundred tents, training marches and all."

"Really? But why?" Fargo mused aloud. "Why set up a private army?"

"For protection?" suggested Oscar.

"I think O'Hagan plans to get rid of the Blackfoot once and for all," said Terrence. "The Blackfoot know it too. They've seen the camp. And those men have been tracking the Indians, ambushing them whenever they can catch them. So the Blackfoot started attacking the wagon trains."

Fargo wondered at Terrence's obvious familiarity with what the Blackfoot thought. Just how friendly was he with the tribe? But he kept silent, filing away the information.

"What about Indians attacking the town?" Fargo asked. "Will they?"

"I doubt it," Terrence said. "The Blackfoot have accepted the fact that there's always going to be a town here. They're just afraid of O'Hagan's army."

"What do you know about Redmond O'Keefe?" Fargo asked.

Terrence swore and spit on the kitchen floor. Oscar winced.

"O'Keefe's famous for his hatred of the English,"

he answered. "And for his hatred of everything that's not Irish green. I've heard he's a swaggering lout who can get men stirred up quicker than a batch of soda bread. Professional troublemaker, that's what he is. Back in Ireland he's become a big hero for blowing up Protestant churches and English army outposts." Fargo heard the mounting anger in Terrence's voice. "Now, I'm not saying the English ought to be in Ireland. Far from it. I'm as Irish as the rest of them. I just think O'Keefe's not trying to find solutions. He's feeding hatred. And what really burns me up is that they're going to take the Indian lands same as the English took over Ireland. They just don't see it's the same thing."

Terrence fell silent, and Fargo leaned back in his chair and thought for a while. Oscar brought them more coffee. Something wasn't adding up right. All of O'Hagan's plotting wasn't about the Blackfoot Indians. Of that he was sure. What was it O'Hagan had said . . . invasion . . . bargaining afterward . . . freeing Ireland? But how could a private army, thousands of miles from Ireland, free Ireland? The answer would come, he knew. He just hoped he could figure it out before it was too late.

"Let's turn in," Fargo said at last. "When Bill gets to the jailhouse in the morning, all hell will break loose."

Early the next morning Skye was feeding Oscar's complete supply of carrots to the two horses in the shed when he heard shouting from the direction of the jailhouse. He slipped out of the shed and back into the photograph gallery. Terrence and Oscar were finishing breakfast.

"They've just found out I've escaped," said Fargo. "If I were Bill O'Hagan, I'd start a house-to-house search immediately. Where can we hide?"

"The closet?" Oscar suggested. Fargo ignored him

and looked about in the gallery for a while, considering various hiding places.

"How about those heavy velvet drapes?" he suggested. "On either side of that backdrop." Terrence nodded agreement.

"Oh!" Oscar said with a start. "That reminds me! I have appointments coming today! I almost forgot about them." He fished a large black ledger from beneath the counter, opened it, and ran his finger down the page. "Oh, yes. Hmm. Fascinating! Mr. Fargo, you'll be interested to know that my first appointment of the day is your intended . . . or Redmond's . . . Miss Bernadette! She's coming for her engagement photograph, I presume. Given the circumstances, I wonder if she'll keep the appointment? If so, she'll be here in a few minutes."

They waited in the gallery, Terrence examining the photographs on the wall, Fargo watching Oscar as he methodically laid out a dozen lenses on the countertop and cleaned them one by one, humming to himself. He was a funny character, Fargo thought. Frightened of his own shadow, perhaps. But Oscar meant well. Of that, Fargo was certain.

They heard shouting out in the street. Fargo signaled Terrence, and they ducked behind the curtains.

"These things are dusty!" Terrence muttered, sneezing.

"Quiet!" Fargo warned. He heard the front door of the gallery open and light footsteps cross the room. He peered out.

The tall slender form of Bernadette O'Hagan crossed the room, her red wavy hair piled loosely on top of her head today and her colorfully plaid dress cut low in the front, exposing her creamy neck.

"Good morning, Oscar."

"I'm surprised to see you today, Miss Bernadette," he answered. They spoke familiarly to one another, Fargo noticed, and he remembered Oscar implying that Bernadette had often come by.

"So, you heard the news about Mr. O'Keefe," she said. "I don't understand what it all means, but I thought I might as well come and have my portrait done today anyway."

"Step right over here," Oscar said. Fargo pulled his head back behind the curtain and waited while Bernadette seated herself on the chair, just a few feet from where he stood. Then he eased the curtain slightly open again so that he could watch. He could see Terrence watching too from behind the other drape. Oscar fiddled with the lens on the camera and then went to the counter, pulling out several jars and mixing together some chemicals, into which he dipped a plate. Then, holding the plate floating in a tray of liquid in front of him, he disappeared under the black cloth at the back of the camera.

"Now, sit tall," he said. "Don't move . . . when I say go, I'll open the shutter. Then remain absolutely still until I tell you when. Go!" Fargo couldn't resist. Noiselessly he eased himself out from behind the curtain to stand motionless in front of the backdrop and behind Bernadette. "Don't move!" Oscar reprimanded her as she jerked, suddenly aware that someone was behind her. It was a long minute and when it was over, Oscar said "Done!" and she whirled about to look at him.

"You!" she exclaimed.

"Look, I'm sorry about yesterday," Fargo said. "I only came into your room to talk to you. Honest." She blushed deep red and looked away.

"I was . . . so worried when I heard they had locked you up!" she murmured. "And then I heard you escaped! But how? Father was furious! And now they're looking for you everywhere! But if you're not Redmond, then who are you anyway?"

Fargo heard the voices out on the street growing louder and doors slamming. The search was coming nearer.

"We haven't got time to talk," he said. "Tell me what your father is planning. What will he do with this army he's raising?"

Bernadette opened her mouth to speak. Fargo heard footsteps on the front stoop. He ducked behind the curtain just as the door flew open.

"Bernadette!" Fargo recognized Bill O'Hagan's voice. Damn. And she had just been about to tell him something.

"Hello, Father," she said. There was the heavy tramp of feet as more men entered the gallery.

"Search everything," O'Hagan said. "I want him found!" For a moment Fargo wondered if Oscar and Bernadette would give them away.

"I . . . I . . . haven't seen anyone," Oscar protested, his voice shaking. "Hey! Be careful with that equipment!" Oscar's voice followed the men into the next room.

"Maybe Redmond's hiding out in the woods," Bernadette suggested. "By the way, Father," she said, her voice slightly louder. "What time is your meeting tonight?" Fargo felt his ears prick up. Bernadette was obviously trying to communicate something to him behind the curtain. Maybe what she had been about to tell him.

"Nine o'clock," O'Hagan snapped. "But don't you be worrying your head about such things, missy. That's no affair of yours."

"Well, I wondered what time you'd be leaving. So I could fix your supper. After all, it's a long ride to that . . . to that old deserted barn on the Sage River." Fargo grinned. She was cool, she was. She had managed to tell him everything. A meeting tonight. What, where, and when. Fargo looked across at Terrence and caught his eye. Terrence nodded thoughtfully.

"Don't be saying the name of Sage River!" O'Hagan hissed quietly so that Oscar would not hear. "Don't ever be saying that name! You never know

94

who might hear it. Get along home with you now. With all the excitement, it's not a day for you to be wandering about."

Fargo heard Bernadette depart. After a few minutes O'Hagan and his men left too. Oscar nervously bid them good-bye. The door shut, and then there came the sound of a heavy thud. Fargo and Terrence peeked out from behind the curtain. Oscar had fainted.

"What happened?" Oscar said, coming around. Fargo had him propped up in the kitchen and loosened his collar.

"Everything's okay," Fargo assured him. "But Terrence and I've got to find a way to get out of town without being discovered."

Oscar got to his feet and shook his head to clear it.

"Wait until night and climb up the cliff," he suggested.

"We can't wait until night," Terrence said impatiently.

"We've got to ride out ahead of them," Fargo explained, "and beat them to the site of this meeting so we can hear what they've got planned. So, we need our horses."

"But how can you walk out the front gate with your horses and not have them recognize you? They'll be watching carefully. Especially today." Oscar said. "What a problem!" He looked thoughtful. "I've got it!" he said at last, looking the two of them over. "It's crazy, but it just might work!"

Fargo watched as Oscar donned his jacket and his hat hurriedly, excitement in his every movement. Then he put the CLOSED sign in his front window and left, saying he'd be back shortly. In fifteen minutes he returned carrying a large carpetbag which he lifted onto the counter. He unbuckled the top and began to remove the contents.

"Women's dresses?" Terrence said, disbelieving. "What good is that?"

Fargo laughed and caught up a wide straw riding hat with a dark heavy veil, placing it on Terrence's head.

"Would you ladies like to go out with me for an afternoon ride?" Oscar asked with a gallant bow.

This will never work, Fargo thought as he surveyed the three of them in the mirror. Terrence and Fargo, dressed awkwardly in the women's dresses with heavy shawls wrapped around them, would never pass inspection. And they towered over Oscar. But if they rode out on their horses, their heights might not be so obvious. And what choice did they have?

"Put your gloves and your veil on, Terrence," Fargo said. "Maybe that will help cover your ugly beard."

"You don't look too pretty either," Terrence smirked, pulling the flowered shawl around his wiry frame.

Oscar disappeared to fetch his horse at the stable, and then they met in the yard in back. Terrence swung up into the saddle.

"Hey!" Fargo called up at him. "Ride sidesaddle, you damn fool!" Fargo swung onto the Ovaro, balancing himself sidesaddle and making sure the skirts and heavy petticoats covered his legs in his Levi's and his boots. It was damned awkward, he thought. How did women ever manage to stay on their horses riding this way? He adjusted the veil over his face. Even with the heavy netting, he'd keep his head down, he decided.

Oscar rode out first, and as they approached the front gate he hailed the men on guard, nervousness in his voice. Fargo raised one gloved hand and wiggled his fingers at one of the guards as they passed. The man whistled back. No accounting for taste, Fargo thought. As they rode through the gate, Fargo kept waiting for shouts or shots to be fired. But all was silent behind them as they rode slowly on the trail between the rolling fields. When they reached the edge of the woods, out of sight of New Dublin, they reined in and dismounted.

"Yee haw!" Oscar shouted excitedly. Fargo smiled at Terrence as they stripped off the women's clothes and donned their own jackets and hats, which had been stowed in the saddlebags.

"We made it! Those stupid suckers!" Oscar jumped up and down and raised one fist in the air.

"Thanks, Oscar," Fargo said, handing him the bundle of rolled-up clothes. "That was a great idea."

"Sure was," Terrence added.

"Let's go. You know the way?" Fargo asked Terrence. O'Shaugnessey nodded assent. "The guards will get suspicious if you return alone so soon," Fargo added, turning toward Oscar. "So stay out here a few hours."

"Stay out here?" Oscar said, suddenly sober, looking around at the silent edge of the woods. "Alone?"

"And when you ride in, tell the guards that your lady friends ran off with some other guys," Terrence suggested. Oscar nodded and swallowed hard.

"You're a good man, Oscar," Fargo added. He put his spur to the Ovaro and followed Terrence as they turned off the trail, galloping into the pine forest. Fargo felt the powerful muscles of the pinto beneath him and the joy the animal felt at being on the open trail again.

They rode through the long afternoon as the wind freshened. Fargo felt the colder moistness in the air that presaged another snow. They galloped along the broad back of a long, forested ridge and then descended the slope. They kept under the trees, only emerging to cross a vast shallow valley, ringed with rounded hills and pied tawny and white, with winter grass and patches of snow. A herd of antelope dotted a bare hillside. In the wide sky above them, clouds gathered, lowered, and turned milky.

Terrence was a good companion on the trail, Fargo thought as he watched the wiry man's form move gracefully with the horse, Indian style. The trapper knew the ways of the wilderness well. Fargo found they established an effortless rhythm as they rode along with an unspoken communication—when to hold back in order to scout out the trail ahead, when to look behind, when to press onward, when to slow down and give the mounts a breather.

By dusk they rode side by side across the open prairie spotted with sage. Ahead Fargo saw a long dark line of low trees.

"That's the Sage River ahead," O'Shaugnessey said, pointing. "The camp's up that way a couple of miles. The barn's there by the river."

"Let's approach through the trees in case anybody's come early," Fargo said. Terrence nodded and they angled off, galloping in a wide circle and entering the trees some distance from the meeting place. They brought the horses to a halt and dismounted under the shelter of the cottonwoods and willows thick on the banks of river.

"We'll go on foot," Fargo suggested. He tethered the Ovaro, stooped down to dip a few handfuls of the cold water, and drank deeply. The horses drank and began to nose at the yellow grasses under the trees.

"It's this way," Terrence motioned, setting off. They hardly made a sound as they moved along the river. A doe nibbled at the bark of a chokecherry and looked up, unconcerned, as they passed by silently in the gathering dusk. The barn came into view. They paused behind a stand of hawthorn saplings and watched for a while. The barn was dark, the open doors gaped below and above. Not far away was a blackened square where a house had once stood, but had been burned down a long time before.

Terrence nodded after a while, and watching all around them, they moved forward into the empty barn. In the dim light it showed signs of recent use. Rude benches, constructed from planks ripped from the barn wall, lined the space on all sides, and the bare earth showed the fresh prints of many booted feet.

"This is the place for sure," Fargo said. He looked around. Where could they secrete themselves in order to hear what was going on? A ladder led up to the second floor. "Let's try that," he said, pointing.

They mounted and found themselves in a large hayloft. There was still a stack of age-darkened bales of hay in the loft, and there were piles of it mounded on the floor. The floor had gaps in places so it would be possible to get a view of the proceedings. This would do very nicely. With the last of the light filtering in through the rotting roof, Fargo and Terrence moved a few of the bales to create a barrier, obscuring them from view should someone ascend the ladder. Then they brought armloads of hay in case they needed further cover. Terrence sneezed violently as they stirred up the dust.

"Hell," he muttered, "this stuff tickles my nose."

Finally there was nothing more to do but wait. Fargo and Terrence positioned themselves behind the bales of hay and near several of the holes in the floor. Fargo fished out a few pieces of jerky, and they chewed in silence. Fargo closed his eyes and napped.

Fargo awoke to the sound of hoofbeats and the jangle of spurs and bridles. It was very dark and cold in the loft. He stretched a little as he listened to the sound of the men's voices as they reined in, surrounding the barn. In a moment he heard the tramp of feet.

"Get the light going," a gruff voice said. A match was struck and flickered out. Then another and a golden light filtered up through the floor. Fargo glanced at Terrence. Tonight they would hear everything the men were planning. If they were lucky. The light increased as the men brought lamps inside and lit them. More men arrived outside. Fargo moved slightly so that he could see down through the hole in the floor. The men were gathering, some already seated on the benches, and the babble of their low voices increased steadily as more arrived and joined the group. Fargo heard the voices of Tommy Fitzgerald as well as Seamus O'Carroll as they greeted other men.

"Have guards been posted?" asked a tight, high voice which rose above the rest, his clipped words betraying him as a military man. "No? You!" he commanded. "And you there! And you and you! Get outside. Keep a sharp eye in all directions. You'll be relieved in an hour."

Another group of men arrived, and Fargo heard a familiar voice. He glanced at Terrence who nodded back.

"Everybody assembled?" O'Hagan boomed as the men quieted. Fargo eased over and saw the large man swagger into the lighted space below and take his place in the center of the room.

"Due to intelligence I have just been receiving, I have an important announcement to make," he said, pausing dramatically. "This will be our last meeting before the invasion!"

The men cheered and whistled below. Fargo watched as O'Hagan smiled and waited for them to quiet down.

"Yes, today I rode up north to meet with our intelligence agent. I'm happy to tell you that we're all clear. The British bastards are camping right on the other side of Chin Coulee. In a couple of days they'll make a fast march up to Edmonton. We'll set out day after tomorrow and move up into position for the assault. By the time they get word and come round, we'll be in full possession of the whole of southern Alberta and half of this territory as well! We'll see how the English imperialists would be liking that!"

The room erupted into cheers and applause. So that was it, Fargo thought, pulling back from the hole. He caught Terrence's eye, and both of them shook their heads simultaneously. It was a mad plan. But it would work. The sparsely populated Canadian province, protected by British garrisons, could be easily taken over by a private army well-positioned at a few key river crossings and mountain passes.

"And, as soon as the English agree to leave Ireland to the real Irish, they can have their precious land back!" O'Hagan added. Fargo smiled in sheer astonishment. O'Hagan planned to hold half a Canadian province ransom for the freedom of Ireland. It was mad, supremely mad. And, damnit, it could work.

"Now, let's be getting our marching orders straight," O'Hagan said. "We'll follow the Indian trail across the border."

"Think them savages will give us any trouble?" one of the men asked.

"Those lily-livered redskins will stay out of our way!" another boasted, and several laughed. "There ain't enough of 'em left to give us much trouble. We've been killing all the ones we've found wandering around." Fargo glanced at Terrence and saw his lips tight with fury.

"Enough!" O'Hagan interrupted. "Now, once we cross the Milk River, O'Neill's unit takes position to patrol the eastern border up to the Red Deer River. O'Carroll's men will head west, taking Fort MacLeod and holding Crowsnest Pass. Fitzgerald and I will head north and take over Calgary. Kavanaugh will head south and form a line of defense halfway across this territory. Now. Here's the important thing. Remember that we're fighting for the freedom of Ireland. Kill every man you see, even if he surrenders! The young ones too. In a few years, remember, they'll be old enough to kill us." Fargo heard murmurs of agreement from the men. "You're a Fenian and don't you be forgetting it! Remember our forefathers, the great heros of Erin and the River Shannon running red with their blood!"

The men cheered again. Fargo shook his head in disgust. How many men would die, how many innocent settlers would lose their lives? How many women would be made widows, and children orphans because of a feud they had nothing to do with on the other side of the ocean?

"What about Redmond O'Keefe?" a voice shouted. "Where's he?"

"Aye! He was supposed to be leading us!" another added.

"Is he a turncoat?"

"Or a yellowbelly?"

"Now, men," O'Hagan shouted, trying to regain control. "If you'll only be keeping quiet, I'll address that very question."

The room became silent. Fargo glanced up at Terrence and saw his nose twitching. Before he could control it, O'Shaugnessey's face contorted as he sneezed violently. The sound reverberated through the stillness of the barn.

6

There was an immediate silence in the room below. Fargo glanced at Terrence. The trapper winced, furious at himself for having sneezed and given away their presence.

"What the hell was that?" said O'Hagan's voice. "There's somebody upstairs." Fargo heard the sound of several pistols being drawn, and he eased away from the hole in the floor as the men looked upward.

Damn, he thought. If they caught Terrence alive, not only would they shoot the trapper, they'd also know he had deceived them and only pretended to shoot Terrence out in the woods. Only one thing to do.

Fargo silently rose to his feet and signaled Terrence to hide himself beneath the straw. He walked swiftly to the ladder and descended. He heard more pistols being drawn.

"Hold your fire," Fargo said.

"It's Redmond!" one of the men closest to the ladder shouted as he came into view.

Fargo paused halfway down and half turned to face the men, holding on to the ladder with one hand. The real Redmond O'Keefe could stir up men, he knew. Stir them up to fight. He'd have to make this good, he realized. Real good.

"How the hell did you get here?" Bill O'Hagan shouted, his face purple with shock.

"I come when Ireland needs me," Fargo said defiantly.

The men muttered and whispered to themselves.

"When I arrived in New Dublin, I wasn't sure about you," Fargo began, without preamble and trying to inflect a little Irish brogue into his voice. "I wasn't sure about any of you. I said to myself, 'they've all gone soft here in America.' I thought you had forgotten all about Ireland. I thought our plans would come to naught because you wouldn't have the will and the guts to fight!" He shook his fist in the air for effect.

"No! Not true!" some of the men protested.

"Wait," Fargo said, raising his hand for silence. "Yes, that's what I told myself: 'Wait. Wait and see what these men are made of. Maybe they haven't gone soft. Maybe they have the will to do what needs to be done.' So I watched the town. And I tested your loyalty. And I asked questions. And I listened. And I even tried out your jail cell!"

Several of the men chuckled.

"And what did I find?" He asked in a tone of accusation. He paused dramatically, looking around the room at each of the men's faces as they shifted uncomfortably, looking up at him perched on the ladder. "Yes, what did I find? I found a town that is as Irish as any on the banks of the River Shannon!"

The men erupted in cheers as Fargo shouted over them.

"I found a group of men willing and able to go to war to free our country! I found an army ready to march, ready to kill, ready to die for Ireland!" He pointed at Bill O'Hagan. "And I found a man who had the vision and the courage to undertake this historic task! Three cheers for Bill O'Hagan!"

The men hurrahed loudly as Fargo led them, and O'Hagan shifted, smiling at the men. That would make it hard for Bill to denounce him now, Fargo thought. He quieted the men.

"Now that I know you are ready, I am honored to be chosen to lead you on this, the greatest conquest of our lives!" The men tried to interrupt with applause, but he continued. "I want you to know that I'll be watching you, waiting for you." As he spoke, Fargo slowly descended the stairs. "In two days' time, in the morning, I will meet you in New Dublin to lead the front guard on to victory." He edged toward a gap in the wall of the barn as he continued to speak. "Until then, my friends and patriots, prepare well for our battle, with the blessing of St. Pat!"

Fargo wheeled and slipped through the gap, out into the open air. The buzz of conversation rose behind him, and he heard several men shouting for him to come back as he bent double and ran quickly around the other side of the barn into a stand of thick rushes. There was no time to lose, he realized. He would have to put as much distance between himself and them as possible, because if they found him, he couldn't keep up the ruse of being Redmond for long. Behind him he heard the men shouting and running out of the barn in confusion, not sure whether to pursue him or not.

He moved almost silently through the stand of rushes until he came to the other side. He peered out into the darkness and saw one of the guards, who had been attracted by the noise, running toward the barn. Fargo froze as the man passed close by. Not far away was a thicket of chokecherry. He pushed into the middle of the tangle and then sank down on his haunches. He doubted that they would search long and hard enough to spot him here.

The men milled about the woods for a while. Then O'Hagan spoke to them—Fargo was too far away to hear the words—and they mounted and rode off, one group in the direction of the camp and the other group riding back to New Dublin. Fargo waited for a while, listening to the silence. He stood, walking quietly out of the thicket and around toward the barn. His eyes pierced the darkness, but he saw no one. He made a soft call, a long series of short whistles like a saw-whet owl. He waited and heard an answer from inside the barn. In another moment O'Shaugnessey was beside him.

"I owe you two," Terrence said. "That was sure fast thinking."

Fargo didn't answer, but nodded in the dark, his thoughts far away. They set out in the direction of their horses, and by the time they arrived Fargo had decided what to do.

"It's five days' ride south to the nearest U.S. Army outpost," Fargo said. "By the time the army chased O'Hagan, he'd be in full possession of the province and half this territory. I'm going to ride up north and find the British garrison," Fargo said. "Maybe if they're warned, they can stop O'Hagan and his men."

"I know the territory. I'll come with you," Terrence said. Fargo nodded. He was hoping the trapper might say that. He was good company on the trail.

They mounted and rode, angling out onto the wide plain, under the starlight. There was no moon. The two dippers hung above the horizon, and they turned slowly during the long night's ride into Canada.

"Chin Coulee is just over there," Terrence said, pointing as they paused at the top of a grassy rise to give their mounts a breather. The sun was just splashing across the low bluffs, patchy with snow.

"And there are the British," Fargo said, pointing to a dim smudge of smoke rising from a distant stand of cottonwoods. They put their spurs to their horses and galloped down the long rise.

The British unit was busy with breakfast. Fargo's keen eyes swept the neat rows of tents pitched among the cottonwoods. At least a hundred men, he thought. Scarcely enough to stop O'Hagan's army, but better than nothing. They were close enough to distinguish the men gathered around the campfires before someone noticed their approach and raised an alarm. A gunshot resounded through the stillness of the morning. Most of the men were still scurrying about retrieving their sidearms as Fargo and Terrence rode into camp.

"Halt!" a high voice shouted.

Fargo and Terrence reined in. A young corporal, his gold buttons gleaming against his red wool jacket, stood with his pistol drawn, aimed at them. Fargo held up his hand to signal their peaceful intentions.

"We've got important news. Who's in charge here?" Fargo said brusquely, ignoring the man's raised pistol. Other men had gathered around, eyeing the strangers curiously.

"That would be Lieutenant Norrington," the man said, lowering his gun. Fargo and Terrence swung down from their mounts, and the corporal signaled them to follow.

Lieutenant Norrington, a rangy and sandy-haired man with a reddish mustache, sat outside his tent at a folding cloth-covered table and scarcely looked up at their approach.

"Lieutenant, sir!" the corporal said, coming to a halt in front of the table and clicking his heels.

"What is it?" Norrington asked, setting down his teacup with an impatient clatter and remaining seated. "Can't it wait until after breakfast?"

"You've got trouble brewing down south," Fargo cut in. "Across the border."

"Anything across the border is not my concern," Norrington said.

"It *will* be your concern," said Fargo. "A man named Bill O'Hagan from New Dublin has raised a private army. Day after tomorrow they plan to march through here and take over the province."

"That's the most absurd thing I've ever heard," Norrington said. "Who are you anyway?"

"Name's Skye Fargo. And this is Terrence O'Shaugnessey."

"Irish, eh?" Norrington said suspiciously, eyeing Terrence.

"That's just the point," said Fargo. "This fellow O'Hagan is leading an army of Irish patriots. After they grab the province, they'll hold it hostage in exchange for the freedom of Ireland."

Norrington looked up at Fargo, and a wide smile spread slowly under his red mustache. Then he chuckled.

"Hold the whole province? Hostage?" he asked, shaking his head. "Ridiculous!" He turned his attention back to his teacup, carefully dropping in two lumps of white sugar. Fargo felt the tiredness of the long night's ride settle on him as he realized the commander didn't believe a word he was saying.

"The only ridiculous thing will be your career if they take this territory away right from under you!" said Fargo. The commander paused in stirring his tea and looked up again at Fargo.

"And how did you come by this information?" Norrington asked coolly.

"I began to suspect a plot when I was staying in New Dublin," Fargo said. "Then I overheard the conspirators outlining the campaign last night in a barn on the Sage River. And O'Shaugnessey here has seen the army camp."

"They have over seven hundred men," Terrence put in. Norrington regarded the trapper slowly, taking in his moccasins, his old slouch hat, his fringed buckskins, and his wiry frame.

"I can smell a green Irishman a mile away," Norrington said. "You may dress like a savage, but you're as Mick as they come. And just why would a shabby Bog-trotter like you be telling me this? If what you're saying is true, then you're betraying your own kind."

Terrence tightened his jaw.

"Look, Norrington," Fargo said, "if you let this Irish army march into Canada, a lot of innocent people—Canadians, British, Americans, Irish—are going to get killed. You've got just enough time to send a man out for reinforcements and to march south. You're outnumbered, but they won't be expecting you, and you might be able to hold them off."

Norrington seemed to give the matter some thought as his pale blue eyes flicked between the two of them. Finally he sighed and took a noisy sip of tea.

"Impossible," he said. "I've got marching orders . . ."

"To go to Edmonton," cut in Fargo.

"Now, how would you know that?" Norrington sputtered.

"The conspirators know it too," Fargo said, his hopes rising. "They're counting on it. As soon as you march out, they'll march in. And they're planning a full-scale slaughter."

Norrington's blue eyes were troubled for just a moment, then he shrugged.

"Ludicrous," he muttered. "You could have guessed our destination. Besides, I have my orders. I can't go chasing some imaginary army just because two strangers, one of them a Mick, come into my camp with some harebrained story. I need proof."

"But . . . but . . ." O'Shaugnessey said. Fargo silenced him with a wave.

"What kind of proof?" Fargo asked hotly. The commander was a fool. Norrington shrugged again.

"How do I know?" he said sarcastically.

"Send one of your own men with us," Fargo suggested. "Then he can ride back and tell you what he's seen."

Norrington considered it for a moment.

"The whole thing is preposterous," he said at last. "And I can't spare one of my men to run off and look at nothing. Corporal, get these men out of camp. Let's have no more interruptions of my breakfast."

Fargo turned on his heel and left, followed by Terrence. As they stalked toward their mounts, the corporal caught up with them.

"Is there really an army of Irishmen down south?" he asked in a worried tone.

"Sure is," Fargo said. "You want to come take a look with us? Then you can ride back and tell your heroic and wise commander."

"I . . . I couldn't do that," the corporal said. "Orders are orders."

"Right," Fargo said. He and Terrence wordlessly mounted and galloped away across the prairie toward the low hills. Fargo felt the anger in him growing. There was no explaining some men's stupidity. Or was it cowardice? Lieutenant Norrington and the British army would be no help at all. And what the hell kind of proof could he bring them? He could just ride away, he realized, far away from the whole sorry mess. It was tempting for a moment. Let Norrington and the goddamn British army lose the province. What the hell did he care? But then he thought of the settlers . . . the ones in Canada and the ones in America . . . who would pay the price of the invasion. Once O'Hagan got his claws into the territory he would be a hard man to dislodge. He was sure of that. But without the help of the British army what kind of chance did they have? Two men against seven hundred. Fargo fell into a black reverie as they pushed their horses onward through the chilly morning, not talking, at one with the wide, open wilderness.

They were well across the border and afternoon was waning before Fargo realized how tired and hungry he was. Although the long hours in the saddle, both the night before and all day, had tired him, he realized the real cause of his exhaustion was that he hadn't decided what to do next. Thoughts of O'Hagan and Redmond O'Keefe swirled in his head along with Lieutenant Norrington, Maureen, and . . . Bernadette. Well, the best ideas often came to him when he was asleep, he thought. O'Shaugnessey was riding loosely in his saddle. He was tired too.

Ahead Fargo sighted a wooded valley, thick with copse. They decided to take cover and get some rest. On the way into the thicket, the horses startled three winter white rabbits. Fargo drew and bagged two of them, missing the third. Weariness was heavy on him. A hot meal and a long nap, he thought over and over.

In a clearing sheltered by tall yellow pines, Fargo laid a quick fire while O'Shaugnessey went to fetch water. Fargo was just bending over to stir the fire when a movement in the underbrush caught his eye. In a flash he realized their mistake. The shots to kill the rabbits had alerted a Blackfoot Indian wandering nearby. In their exhaustion, they had neglected to scout out the area before camping. Damn, he thought. They had behaved as recklessly as tenderfeet.

He tensed, turned, and drew the Colt, but the Indian lurking in the brush ducked behind a log. And six others, two with rifles, four with bows drawn, advanced on him from all sides, murder in their faces.

Fargo calculated his chances in a split second. He was standing in the middle of the clearing with no cover nearby. He didn't have a chance, and the best he could do was to take one of two with him. One of the Indians tightened his grip on his rifle, giving Fargo a split second to realize he was going to shoot. He jumped sideways as the rifle exploded, the shot zinging by his ear.

"Stop! Friend!" Fargo heard in Algonquian, as he rolled once on the ground coming to a halt with his Colt at the ready. "He is my friend!" he heard again in the Indian tongue used by many of the tribes, the Blackfoot among them. The warriors lowered their weapons. Fargo looked in the direction of the voice as O'Shaugnessey emerged from the brush.

"You're back just in time," Fargo said.

The braves smiled and nodded at Terrence, lowering their rifles and loosening their bows, returning the arrows to their otterskin quivers. Fargo slowly holstered his pistol as he watched Terrence warmly embrace one of the Blackfoot, a young well-muscled brave with white painted stripes on his face and a prominent nose.

"This is Ravenbeak," Terrence said to Fargo.

Fargo introduced himself and greeted the brave in his own language. Both men started to hear him speak Algonquian.

"You speak the Indian tongue well," Ravenbeak said to Fargo. "And you are a friend of Hair-On-Face," he added, nodding at the grizzled Terrence. Fargo grinned at the trapper's Indian name. O'Shaugnessey was obviously very close to the tribe to warrant his own name.

"They thought you were one of the men from O'Hagan's camp," O'Shaugnessey explained in English. "They were out for revenge because some of the men slaughtered a hunting party a couple of days ago."

Ravenbeak looked quizzically from one to another as they spoke in English. Fargo had a sudden thought.

"Do you think they might help us?" he asked Terrence. The trapper shrugged.

"Maybe," he said, glancing at Ravenbeak, who continued to listen to their conversation carefully, even though he did not understand the white man's tongue. "They're plenty angry about the killings."

"Come and eat with us," Fargo said in Algonquian. He pointed to the rabbits lying near the fire.

Ravenbeak smiled slowly, looking down at the two rabbits and up at the other six men. He nodded.

"Skye is gracious to share the little food," he answered. "We will bring more white ones."

The braves disappeared into the woods, and Terrence and Fargo set to building up the fire. They returned shortly with at least a dozen rabbits and a few ring-necked pheasants.

"We will feast," Fargo said approvingly to Ravenbeak. "Blackfoot are good hunters." The warrior smiled widely at the compliment.

While Fargo put on a large pot of coffee, the Blackfoot quickly skinned the hares and plucked the birds, tearing the joints into pieces. Terrence fetched some long roasting sticks which he whittled to a point.

Soon they sat in a circle around the fire, passing around the two tin mugs of hot steaming coffee, which delighted the Indians, and holding the sizzling gobbets of meat over the roaring yellow flames.

As the afternoon passed and dusk began to fall, the braves took turns telling tales of the Old Man who defeated the enemies under the lake, and of the Thunderbird whose flashing eyes made lightning and whose flapping wings made thunder.

Fargo listened and ate, sitting next to Ravenbeak and watching him closely, trying to take his measure and come up with a plan. Could the Indians help them stop O'Hagan and his men? The reckless slaughter of their hunting parties by O'Hagan's army gave them every reason to seek revenge. But Indians were unpredictable. It would be a delicate matter to ask them to help in a white man's battle. And, Fargo realized, if they attacked O'Hagan's army before they crossed the border into Canada, he would be guilty of inciting the Indians. But the Blackfoot didn't recognize the border between Canada and the United States. To them, land existed not for ownership, but as an unbroken and free place for wandering and hunting. The Indians could not understand how the white man could say that he owned land. So, it would be a difficult matter to explain what O'Hagan's army was up to.

From the attitudes of the other braves, Fargo deduced that Ravenbeak was one of the leaders of the tribe—perhaps the son of the chief. And the young brave was watching him covertly too, Fargo noticed. At last all the meat had been roasted and eaten, and the group reclined around the warm fire.

"You, Skye, have a question in your eyes," he said, not looking at him. "Perhaps sacred smoke will loosen your tongue."

"I am honored," Fargo said as he watched Ravenbeak signal one of the braves to bring over a deerskin pipe bundle. He recognized the distinctive design of tadpoles and hailspots. The Blackfoot did not often open their pipe bundles before strangers. Clearly, he had passed a test of some kind.

Ravenbeak began a quiet chant as he spread a piece of skin on the rock beside him and removed bird skins, a bead necklace, and several small dark objects that looked like dried animal organs. Finally, he drew forth a long pipe. He carefully filled it with tobacco, lit it with a flaming brand from the fire, drew in a long puff, and then passed it, ceremoniously, to Fargo.

Skye took it carefully, pausing to admire the feathers hanging from the stem and to point approvingly at the small figures of running animals drawn on the bowl. He must follow the customs, he thought. Not appear too eager to ask his question. The Indians did not admire, and in fact mistrusted, eagerness.

After the pipe had made the first round of the circle, Ravenbeak broke the silence.

"You and Hair-On-Face have ridden hard," he observed handing the pipe again to Fargo.

"We went north to find help," Fargo said, "against the white men camped by the Sage River."

Ravenbeak nodded thoughtfully and there was a long pause.

"Did you find help in the north?" he asked.

"No," Fargo said. "The other white men did not believe that the Sage River men would come to take their land."

Ravenbeak thought for another moment, his eyes closed.

"If the Sage River men go north, they will leave this land," he said.

"No," Terrence cut in. "They will not leave. They will take more land here. And more white men like them will come."

"I do not understand white men," Ravenbeak said, his eyes opening again. "They want to take land. They want to take all the land. But land does not want to be taken." He shook his head sadly. "Another thing," he said. "Why do you fight these men, Skye? Do you want to take land too?"

Fargo looked into the Indian's black eyes. Hell, he thought. Why was he suddenly in the middle of somebody else's war? Once again he thought about turning his back, riding away. But then, what would happen? Bill O'Hagan would seize most of this territory and half the Canadian province. He'd kill every male settler he found. And every Blackfoot, male or female or child.

"No, I don't want land," Fargo said. "I want peace."

Ravenbeak grunted.

"In my time there is no peace in the three worlds," he said, shaking his head. "Not here, not under the lake, not beyond the sky dome. But it is a great warrior who fights for no fighting. Still, there are many Sage River men," he observed.

"Many," said Fargo. "And there are two of us," he added, nodding across the fire toward Terrence. This

115

was the moment that the Indian would offer help. Or wouldn't.

"Two are not enough to win the battle," said Ravenbeak. He looked sad and cleaned out his pipe carefully. He slowly began to replace his sacred objects into the parfleche, not looking at Fargo.

"You have many strong warriors," Terrence said. Clearly, even as close as he was to the tribe, the trapper could not directly ask the Blackfoot to join him in battle.

Ravenbeak did not answer, but finished repacking his pipe bundle and folded over the flap. Fargo's hopes sank as the brave got to his feet and the others stood as well.

"In the time of my father's father," Ravenbeak said, "our people hunted many many buffalo. There were so many that they were like dark clouds on a rainy day, passing on the plain." Fargo listened patiently, wondering where this was leading. He trusted that Ravenbeak was not just telling a meaningless tale. "The tribe had much meat, many skins, many horns. No white men. No one taking land."

"A time of peace," Fargo said, nodding. Ravenbeak smiled.

"Yes, peace," he agreed. "There were so many buffalo that they even wanted to be killed by the Blackfoot. We did not use our bows. We did not ride on the big dogs to chase them. Instead, we said a prayer to the Thunderbird. And we followed the great buffalo north to a place called Estipah-Siki-Kini-Kots. A sacred place where the buffalo went to die for the Blackfoot. But now there are few buffalo and too many white men. Maybe the two warriors should learn this prayer to the Thunderbird." Fargo felt confused. What was the story about?

"Estipah-Siki-Kini-Kots?" Fargo repeated slowly. The Algonquian words were familiar and he tried to translate them.

"Something about 'his head,' " said Terrence in English.

"And the word *smash*," said Fargo, trying the Indian words out again.

"Place . . . where . . . his head . . . is smashed!" Terrence said. "Or, Place-where-he-got-his-head-smashed."

"Sounds promising," said Fargo in English. "Where is this sacred place?" Fargo asked Ravenbeak in Algonquian.

The brave knelt and picked up a stick, drawing a river with branches, some round curves for mountains, then a kind of triangle. O'Shaugnessey came around to watch.

"I know that area," he said as the brave drew the map. "It's up between Longbow Coulee and McIver's Gap. There's a long hill with a wide old Indian trail on top between two wooded slopes. I never followed it all the way." The Indian continued to draw.

"The buffalo run here," he said, pointing. "Then they go here between the trees." He indicated an area between two lines that narrowed toward a point. "At the end . . ." He made a motion with his hand and fingers to indicate the buffalo running and then falling a long distance to land on the ground.

"Cliff?" Fargo asked in Algonquian.

"Big smash heads," said Ravenbeak, smiling. He tossed down the stick and stood suddenly and raised his hand, uttering the farewell. Terrence and Fargo made the farewell responses. The Blackfoot slipped out of the clearing quietly, mounted, and were gone.

"Estipah-Siki-Kini-Kots . . ." Terrence repeated, looking down at the marks in the earth. "I've been around here for twenty years and no Blackfoot has ever mentioned that place. It's that sacred to them."

"I guess the cliff can't be seen until you're right on top of it," Fargo said. "It's interesting. But it's one thing to get a herd of buffalo to run blindly off a cliff. I doubt a bunch of professional fighters is going to

117

stampede. But, what the hell," he added, half to himself, "it's the best chance we've got."

It was too dark to move on. Fargo fetched a load of wood for the fire and their bedrolls. They drew close to the warm flames and fell asleep. Fargo dreamed of running buffalo. On the back of one rode a slender naked girl with long wavy red hair.

At dawn they reined in their mounts on the hill overlooking New Dublin, staying well inside the perimeter of the woods so that they couldn't be seen. They had been riding for three hours.

Smoke rose from the chimneys of the walled town, and the sentries walked back and forth on top of the wall. Men scurrried about in the streets, packing saddlebags and loading wagons.

"Stay out of sight," Fargo said to Terrence. "Keep your eye on the town and follow the army when we set out for Canada. If I need to, I'll send you smoke signals. If I can. Then if I can get them up to that cliff . . . well, I don't know exactly how we're going to do it . . ."

"But I'll be hanged if Bill O'Hagan is going to win this one!" Terrence said.

Fargo swung out onto the trail and descended toward the walled town. This morning the waterwheel turned slowly. The waterfall had iced over during the cold night. When he approached the front gate the sentries shouted to one another excitedly.

"He's here!" one exclaimed.

"Open the gate!"

"Get the men ready! Get our guns!"

Fargo paused as the massive wooden gates swung slowly open, and then he rode the pinto into the town. The gates shut behind him. Men were running out of the buildings to gather on the sidewalks to watch him pass. Damn, he thought. Here it goes again. The Redmond O'Keefe act. If he could just keep up the ruse a little longer. . .

He rode through the streets of New Dublin toward Bill O'Hagan's house as men followed, muttering quietly, a large crowd gathering and swelling behind him. He reined in before the stone house, dismounted, and tethered the Ovaro. A curtain flickered at the window. The heavy wooden door opened and Bill O'Hagan filled the doorway.

"Well, well!" he exclaimed, his triple chin shaking. "Mr. Redmond O'Keefe! Hero of Ireland! I thought you'd run away after we saw you on the Sage River. Welcome back to New Dublin." Fargo didn't like O'Hagan's tone, but he ignored it. Sound like Redmond O'Keefe, he told himself.

"You can always count on me," he replied to O'Hagan. "I am ready to lead us all to victory, as soon as you and your men are ready to go."

"Oh, we're ready to go," said O'Hagan. "All of us true Irishmen in New Dublin are ready to fight. But I'm not sure we want to be following you, now do we?" He stepped out of the doorway.

He was followed immediately by a second man, who stepped onto the stoop. Fargo looked into the face of the real Redmond O'Keefe.

7

Fargo narrowed his eyes as he regarded the man standing before him. So, at long last, this was Redmond O'Keefe.

"Grab him boys," O'Hagan hissed. Two men seized his arms and held him. Fargo didn't resist. With the crowd around him, there was no immediate chance for escape.

Redmond was shorter than he was, Fargo noted, which didn't show in the photographs. And he wasn't as broad in the shoulders, but was more compact. He wore a cutaway jacket, European-style, and a linen vest, and carried a wide black felt hat in one hand. Fargo studied the man's face, comparing it with his own. Redmond's beard was clipped more neatly and his jawline was wider. But it was the eyes that Fargo didn't recognize as his own. They glittered with a kind of suppressed and watchful passion that threatened at any moment to turn violent. But the resemblance was close and uncanny.

O'Keefe must have arrived the day before, Fargo thought, while he and Terrence had been riding up to Canada. And O'Keefe and O'Hagan had had plenty of time to figure out that there had been an imposter. Damn, he thought, searching for a way to turn the situation around. He'd be lucky to get out alive. He had a sudden inspiration.

"I sure am glad to see you!" Fargo said innocently to his double. O'Hagan's bushy brows shot up in surprise, and O'Keefe regarded him warily. "It was getting damned hard to play the part of the hero when I'm just a nobody." He'd have to lay this on thick to get away with it, he thought.

"What would you be jabbering about?" Redmond said stiffly. "Nobody told you to lie about being me."

"The hell they didn't!" said Fargo. "As soon as I got to New Dublin everybody started calling me O'Keefe. I told them and told them that I wasn't you, but nobody listened."

"That's true," cut in Fitzgerald. "He kept saying his name was something else . . ."

"Shut up!" O'Hagan snapped.

"Finally, when I realized how much they were all looking forward to the great Redmond O'Keefe coming and helping them," continued Fargo, "I just couldn't disappoint them. So, I played along, figuring when you—the real Redmond O'Keefe—got here, we'd straighten it out, and I could go along with my business."

Fargo noted that the men standing around relaxed slightly, nodding to themselves. Some of them were buying his story. Hell, it wasn't too far from the truth.

"Then who are you?" Redmond asked, his glittering dark eyes fixed on him.

"The name's Skye Fargo. People call me the Trailsman."

"You'd be hiring yourself out to make a living?" Redmond said. "Is that it?"

Fargo thought fast. Now, if O'Keefe would hire him to lead them to Canada . . .

"Sure," he said. "I break trails. Find the fastest, safest way to any place you want to go. You in the market?"

"You listened to our meeting at the old barn," growled O'Hagan. "You know damned well . . ."

"Wait," said O'Keefe. He looked Fargo up and down slowly. "Now I know your name and your occupation. You still haven't told me who you are." Fargo shrugged.

"I break trails," he said.

Redmond considered his answer for a moment.

"And your loyalties?" he asked. "The test of a man is what he's willing to die for. For his religion or for his country. It's what makes him a man. What do you believe in?"

"I'm loyal to myself," answered Fargo. "That's enough for me." But it gets me in a lot of trouble, he added to himself.

"This man is unpredictable and dangerous," O'Keefe said quietly to O'Hagan, but purposely loud enough so that Fargo would overhear. "But possibly useful to us. Hire him. But keep an eye on him."

"Happy to be of help," Fargo said as the men holding him released their grips. Just then they heard a voice, a female voice, screaming at the top of her lungs.

"Where the hell is he, the rotten bastard?" With a sinking heart, Fargo recognized the voice as Maureen's.

She came running up the street from the direction of the mill, carrying a small sack of flour over her shoulder. She pushed her way to the center of the group until she saw Fargo and Redmond standing side by side.

"This bastard!" she said. "This low-down skunk came awooing me claiming to be Redmond O'Keefe! I demand . . ."

"I told you I wasn't O'Keefe. But you didn't listen," he shouted back at her. "And, anyway, why were you encouraging your sister's fiancé?" Maureen stopped, her mouth gaping at him, her dark eyes flashing fury.

"You said it was me you would marry!" she said, collecting herself. She wasn't above lying to gain the advantage, Fargo realized. "Yes, you said you were Redmond O'Keefe and you wanted to marry me and not Bernadette. You and your sweet and false words! And now I demand that he be punished!"

"Now, Maureen," O'Hagan said gruffly. "You're being just a little worked up."

"I'm not!" she said, her hysterics getting the better of her.

"That'll teach you to lead on strangers," O'Keefe said firmly. "Especially ones who aren't patriots."

"Listen to your future brother-in-law and do what he says," O'Hagan added.

Maureen's face turned purple with fury at the public rebuke. She wheeled away, shooting Fargo a look of murderous rage. He was suddenly very glad to be leaving town.

Just then there was a stir at the door and Bernadette stepped out. The early morning light made her snowy skin look all the more transparent, her long red hair encircling her face. But Fargo also noticed the deep black circles under her eyes. In one hand she held a rolling pin, and flour dusted her apron. She caught Fargo's eye and jumped with surprise, then smiled slowly. He saw tears start in her eyes, and she turned away to go back into the house.

"Come here, Bernadette," O'Keefe called. She came forward and stood beside him, looking at the ground. "This man doesn't look much like me, does he?" O'Keefe asked her. "Look at him. Which of us do you prefer?" His voice was taunting, hard-edged. She shrugged and refused to look up, looking down at her rolling pin. Fargo could imagine what she was thinking. "Get into the house," O'Keefe said, seizing her arm roughly and pushing her toward the doorway.

"She just needs a very firm hand by a strong man," O'Keefe said to O'Hagan.

"That she does," Bill agreed, slapping him on the back. O'Hagan was obviously impressed by O'Keefe and was happy to let him take control of some things. Like his daughter.

"It's getting late," O'Keefe said, looking up at the bright sky. "We should have left by now! Let's get going."

Fargo found himself in the middle of a roiling mass of men getting their horses, wagons, and gear assembled in columns on the main street. He led his Ovaro toward the head of the column and waited patiently, amazed at his own good luck. This just might work, he thought. If he could lead the army toward the cliff . . .

Fargo thought about it as he tightened the cinch on the Ovaro and inspected the fastenings on the saddlebags. He heard shouting from the direction of the gate and noticed, out of the corner of his eye, the doors slowly opening; several men on horses rode through, and then the doors closed again. He mounted and rode over beside O'Hagan and O'Keefe. This, he thought, was going just fine.

He turned his attention to the several men who had just ridden through the front gate. They rode up the street toward the column. Behind them they were dragging something, which was hidden by their horses.

When they came close, they moved their horses to either side, exposing to view the bound and gagged man they were dragging up the street.

"Mr. O'Hagan. Look who we found lurking out in the woods," one of the men said. "None other than Terrence O'Shaugnessey."

O'Hagan's jaw dropped as he looked down at the trapper, who groaned and stirred. He was still alive, Fargo noticed, and his buckskins had kept him from being torn up as they dragged him along. Still, he looked like he'd been beaten pretty badly.

"What the hell?" O'Hagan roared, his face coloring pink, then deep red. Fargo's thoughts whirled. He measured the distance to the front gate, which was now closed. If he rode up to it . . . but he'd be shot in the back before he got ten yards down the street.

He watched as O'Hagan blinked several times, the thought slowly dawning on him. He turned in fury toward Fargo. "You bastard," he shouted. "You dirty, lying, stinking bastard. You didn't kill O'Shaugnessey at all. You'll pay for this!"

Several of the men nearby seized the pinto's bridle. In a flash Fargo drew his Colt. But there were twenty men around him who had their guns at the ready in an instant. All pointed directly at him. If he fired, he'd be dead in an instant. Damn. It had been going so well.

He handed the pistol over and slid down off the Ovaro. His thoughts whirled, and he tried to think of a way to talk himself out of this one, but his culpability was too obvious. They pinioned his arms and tied them behind him.

"What's going on?" O'Keefe asked while they were securing Fargo. O'Hagan filled him in quickly on the execution of O'Shaugnessey out in the woods. Fargo strained against the ropes, twisting them to see if he could get his hands free, but they were tightly bound.

"And who's this man, O'Shaugnessey?" He motioned toward the inert figure in the street.

"Trapper," O'Hagan answered. "From Ireland. A lot of trouble. Been living with Indians for twenty years now."

"He might be useful," O'Keefe said, looking down from his horse at Terrence. O'Hagan opened his mouth to protest, but then thought better of it. "In any case, I'd like to question him about the Indian situation. He might give us some useful information on how to kill them off. Afterwards, we'll be disposing of him. Tie him onto a horse and he'll come with us. As for you, Mr. Fargo," Redmond said, turning to look down at him, "you're lying about something. But I don't have time to find out what or why."

"Death is too good for the likes of him!" Maureen said, pushing forward from the crowd.

"Right you are, Maureen. So you can decide how he dies," O'Keefe said with a wave of his hand. Maureen's face lit up. "Fitzgerald will stay behind and help you. Just make sure he's completely dead. Now, let's get going."

Fitzgerald dismounted and grabbed Fargo's arm. All around them the men of New Dublin formed their columns of horses and wagons and rode out. On the sidewalks the women waved their handkerchiefs in the air. Fargo heard Maureen and the other women singing the familiar song:

We'll crush our foes like grain . . .
There'll be blood in the bread
Of our dear Ireland!

After the last man passed the town wall, the gates shut slowly. Maureen turned toward Fargo, humming the song.

"Now, how should I let you die?" she mused, looking him over. "Shoot you? Oh, that's much too quick."

"I'm a lot more fun alive," Fargo said. "But then, you know that perfectly well."

"Don't you be insulting the lady!" Fitzgerald said, shaking him by the arm. Maureen hummed again and her face brightened.

"I've got it!" she said, her face brightening. "Follow me."

She led the way through the street, and they approached the mill, with the waterwheel turning very slowly under the partially frozen falls. She entered, and Fitzgerald pushed Fargo inside.

"Tie him to that," Maureen said, pointing at the horizontal stone wheel that slowly revolved under the second one to mill the grain. "It will be just like in the song," she said.

She hummed the tune again as Fitzgerald pushed

him against the wheel. This was the moment, Fargo thought. He was bound, but if he could just get Tommy down on the ground and reach the Arkansas toothpick in his ankle sheath . . . Fargo kicked out, but Tommy dodged and shouldered him. Fargo fell back onto the stone wheel, his head hitting the stone. The ceiling whirled with stars for a moment, and then he saw nothing.

Fargo struggled up through the layers of blackness, blinking his eyes. The room spun and then slowly came into focus. In an instant he remembered where he was, and he surged against the ropes tight across his chest. It was too late. He was firmly tied onto the giant millstone, which moved slowly toward the crushing stone. He glanced over at Maureen and Fitzgerald, who were talking and ignoring him for the moment. He contracted his body against the restraints, but he couldn't reach the knife at his ankle. The stone moved slowly. Six feet more before it began to crush him. He pushed against the ropes again. No chance. He glanced again at the pair talking. Tommy turned his head suddenly toward the door.

"I hear something outside," he said. "I'll be back."

"I'll be sitting right here watching," she said, noticing Fargo's attention. "Looks to me like you're going to lose your left foot first."

Fargo raised his head and measured again the distance to the grinding stone. Because of the angle he was tied, his left foot would go under the stone first. Then his leg, hips, right leg, and torso. His arms and head would go last, he realized. He wondered how long he would feel the pain before he died. Goddamn.

"Let me go, Maureen," he tried. "I told you I enjoyed our night together. We could have a lot more like that one."

"Nice try, Fargo," she said. "But, no. I'm going to enjoy this. I've never seen a man crushed to death before." Fargo stared at her. It was hard to believe that the soft and willing Maureen was capable of such cruelty. But he saw her face harden and the eyes shine with anticipation.

"I'm going to make a real mess of this stone," Fargo said. "There must be a better way to kill me." One yard left, he noticed. He shifted his left leg as far away from the crushing stone as he could.

"We've got plenty of water to wash the stone off afterward," Maureen said, humming the song again. Goddamnit, he thought, trying to reach the ankle knife again. But O'Shaugnessey had tied him too tightly. Two feet to go. His thoughts whirled.

"I've got some information you might be interested in," said Fargo. "It's about the British garrison up in Canada." That might work. He could make up something to scare her.

"I don't believe you," said Maureen. "You just want to trick me, but you won't!" She covered her ears with her hands and began to sing the song again. Fargo lifted his head again. One more foot to go. His booted foot was as far as he could pull it away from the huge grinding stone that now loomed over him. And in another moment he would lose his foot, his leg, and his life.

Just then he heard a sound at the door. He lifted his head and looked beyond Maureen, who was still holding her hands over her ears and singing. She had heard nothing. The door squealed open and still she continued to sing. Fargo kept his face impassive as he saw Bernadette slip inside the door. The rolling pin was in her hand, and she was sneaking up behind her sister. Fargo felt the stone against his left boot. He strained against the rope again and managed to move it away another inch.

Maureen suddenly stopped singing and opened her mouth to say something. Bernadette, her rolling pin raised and her eyes wide with terror, hesitated.

"Hit her!" Fargo shouted. His words galvanized

her, and before Maureen could move or utter a word she brought the rolling pin down on the back of her sister's head. Not hard enough to kill her, Fargo noted, as Maureen sagged to the ground. Fargo felt the stone against his boot again. This time he could not move his leg any further away.

"Help me!" he shouted. Bernadette came running. In a panic she pushed the rolling pin under the crushing stone. It forced the stones apart slightly, but didn't halt the motion. The stone was grinding away Fargo's left boot and he could feel the roughness against his skin. "Get the knife on my right ankle," he instructed her.

In a flash she had removed the knife and sawed at the rope holding his left leg down. Fargo felt the stone grinding his foot. In another moment, it would be crushed. Just then, the rope gave way and he pulled his leg free.

"My hands," he said. She freed his hands, and he took the knife from her, quickly slicing the other ropes and rolling off the millstone to land on his feet. Fargo looked down at his left foot. One side of the boot had been worn away by the stone and some of his skin as well. But what the hell. He had all five toes left. And his life.

"Thank you," he said, looking up at Bernadette. Her face dissolved in tears, and he put his arms around her slenderness.

"I would have . . . felt so terrible," she said between sobs, "if something had . . . happened to you. And this whole war . . . is so wrong. I've always felt that way, but . . . I felt so alone."

He tightened his arms around her as she clung to him, her chest heaving. Her small breasts pushed against him as he held her close, and her sobs gradually subsided. He continued to hold her. She was tall, her head resting on his shoulder, but his hands easily spanned her narrow waist. He felt himself aroused. Oh, hell, he thought. If they only had time.

Bernadette pulled away slightly, wiping her face with her hands, and looked up into his eyes. Fargo leaned over and brushed her soft lips with his. She smiled and he kissed her again, deeply, her lips parting to welcome his exploring tongue.

This is crazy, Fargo thought to himself as he tasted her sweetness and let his hands rove over her slender form. There was Maureen out cold on the floor. She could awaken any moment. And where the hell was Fitzgerald? And what of O'Shaugnessey, held hostage by O'Hagan's men as they marched into Canada? Still, he continued to kiss Bernadette, tangling his hands in her thick wavy hair, sculpting the curve of her waist with his hands. And she responded, her breath coming in short gasps, her hands clutching his broad muscled back.

"There's no time," he murmured into her hair.

"I know," she said. "But I want you like I've never wanted anyone else. And we may never have a second chance." She paused, and her frank blue eyes met his. "Come. Please." She took his hand and led him through a small door in the wall into a small room with mounds of hay on the floor. She shut the door behind her, bolted it, and turned.

Fargo seized and kissed her, feeling her hands fumble with his shirt buttons. He swiftly undid the buttons on the back of her dress, and she slipped it down around her waist. He slid his hand under her camisole and felt her shiver as he massaged the small hard nipple of her breast.

"Yes, yes," she murmured. "Oh, Skye . . ."

They sank down onto the prickly, fragrant hay as he pulled down her camisole, exposing her small white breasts with the delicate pink nipples. He kissed them, playing his tongue over their erectness as she groaned, and her hands felt for the buttons of his Levi's. She slipped her hand downward and gasped as she felt his huge rod. He pulled down his Levi's as she struggled out of her bloomers. He touched the soft inside of her thigh as he kissed her, trailing his fingers upward.

"Yes, please take me," she moaned. "I want you so."

Skye felt her warm fur, and then he slipped his finger gently into her deep wetness. She shivered.

"Yes," she whispered. "More." He slowly slipped another finger into the smooth tightness of her, pushing against the slight resistance until he felt it give. She groaned.

"Please, come inside me," she whispered.

"Not yet," he said. He bent over her and nuzzled her, inhaling the sweet muskiness of her odor, darting his tongue out to flick across her. She moaned and writhed on the hay as he took her completely into his mouth, sucking and flicking her with his tongue.

"Ah . . . ah!" she screamed, then tried to stifle her own cries as she moved up and down in ecstasy. "Oh . . . stop . . . stop . . . no . . ." He continued, until he felt her contractions becoming nearly unbearable, and she came suddenly, with a violent shudder. He straightened and kissed her.

"Oh, my god!" she said. "Oh, Skye. I never knew . . ."

"Like that?" he asked.

"Oh . . ." she said, unable to answer. "Please. Now, come inside me." She reached down to grasp his largeness, and he slowly eased inside her, pausing as she widened gradually to take him in. Finally, he began moving with long strokes and felt her warm tightness around him. He pulled her knees up on either side of him and pushed against her.

"Oh, oh . . ." she moaned again. "Oh, yes. I think it's going to happen again . . ." He felt her clutch his back as he plunged deeply into her again, again. Her face contorted suddenly, and he gave himself up to her, feeling the fire gathering at the base and erupting upward, deeply into her as she came again. He fell forward on top of her and felt her arms hold him.

"Mmmm," she murmured after a time. "You're . . . wonderful. It was my . . . my first time."

"I know," he said, kissing her hair. "You were wonderful too." She smiled shyly at the compliment. "I'd like to stay all afternoon," he said, rolling off of her and coming to his feet. "But I have to get going. A man's life is at stake."

"Terrence O'Shaugnessey?" she asked, pulling on her bloomers and pulling down her skirts.

"Exactly. Now, I'm going to need some help getting out of town. I need you to bring my horse—the black-and-white one—out to the front gate. Then you'll have to distract them." He told her his plan and she left quickly, while he waited in the mill.

Maureen was still out cold on the floor. Bernadette had given her a good whack with the rolling pin, but she was breathing deeply and there was only a purple bruise on her forehead. Nothing that a little time wouldn't fade. One thing that wouldn't fade was her need for revenge, he realized. He hoped she wouldn't figure out who had knocked her out. But if he succeeded in stopping O'Hagan and O'Keefe, she would be safe, he realized.

He went to the door of the mill and cracked it open. A few feet outside, half hidden behind some bags of grain, he saw Fitzgerald, also out cold. Bernadette was a lot braver than she seemed, he thought. Just then he saw a familiar figure scurrying by.

"Oscar!" he half whispered. The little man stopped at the sound of his name and looked about. Fargo had a sudden idea. "Oscar!" he called again. Oscar sighted him, and his pale skin turned even paler.

"You again!" he said, walking over reluctantly. "I thought they were . . . killing you."

"They tried," Fargo said, opening the door and motioning him inside out of sight.

"Look, I need your help again," Fargo said.

"More dresses?" Oscar asked. In spite of himself, the photographer chuckled, remembering how they had sneaked out of town. "And after I got you out, you left me in the woods as thanks?"

"But you survived it," Fargo pointed out. Oscar nodded. "Now I want you to ride out with me. We're going after O'Hagan's army," Fargo said.

"How can I possibly help?" Oscar said nervously. "I have a pistol, but I'm not a very good shot."

"I have a feeling you can shoot just fine," Fargo said. "I want you to bring your camera."

8

Fargo ducked down behind a stack of barrels near the main gate as he watched the guard on top of the parapet. Most of the men of New Dublin were off with O'Hagan, and there was only one guard at the gate. Oscar Wyndham came into view, leading two horses, one loaded with his bulky camera equipment. The little photographer approached the wooden barrier and called to the guard, who climbed down the ladder to unbolt the doors.

Bernadette appeared, leading the Ovaro. The pinto smelled Fargo nearby and whinnied low. Fargo peered over the barrels and saw Bernadette's questioning look at seeing Oscar there. But Oscar turned his back to the guard and put his finger to his lips, and she nodded, understanding that he was in on the scheme to get Fargo out of the town. As she walked toward the gate, she idly dropped the Ovaro's bridle and approached the guard, who had his back turned, preparing to open the gate. As he swung open the first huge wooden door, it obscured Fargo from the guard's view. Fargo bent double and slipped past the open door, ahead of Oscar. The pinto, sighting and smelling him, moved forward at a trot through the gate.

Fargo leapt onto the horse's back and galloped away, hoping that the hoofbeats on the earthen trail wouldn't attract the guard's attention. He knew that Bernadette was finding some way to keep the man distracted. The only hitch would be if the guard noticed that the pinto pony had disappeared. He turned in his saddle to look back.

Oscar had stopped his horses just at the entrance of the gate, blocking the second door from being opened. Fargo turned his attention to riding up the hill as quickly as possible, the Ovaro's smooth muscles strong beneath him. At the edge of the woods and almost out of sight of the town, he stopped and turned to look back again.

The gate was just closing behind Oscar, who climbed up into his saddle and trotted along toward Fargo. He joined him in a few minutes.

"Thanks, Oscar," Fargo said.

"Don't thank me," said the photographer. "Bernadette kept thinking up all kinds of excuses why she needed the guard to look this way and then that. Luckily, he was real dumb." Oscar chuckled to himself.

"Let's go. We've got a hard ride ahead of us," Fargo said. "Let's catch up with O'Hagan's army."

Fargo set a slow pace at first, watching to see if Wyndham would be able to keep up. But the photographer did fine, although he bounced around a lot. Still, he didn't complain.

By midafternoon Fargo reined in. Oscar rode up beside him. Fargo studied the ground in front of him.

"Interesting," he said.

"What?"

"I would have thought that the men from Sage River would have marched out to meet the New Dubliners. It would have saved them time. But instead, O'Hagan and O'Keefe and his men are heading toward the camp. And they're not hurrying." Oscar examined the hoofprints in the mud before them.

"You can tell all that from this mud?" he asked. Fargo nodded, deep in thought. "Amazing," Oscar added.

"That means they've decided to stay the night at

Sage River Camp and march tomorrow. That could be better for us. We'll need daylight. Come on." Before Oscar had a chance to ask for an explanation, Fargo galloped off, following the wide track left by the New Dubliners.

Fargo and Oscar lay hunched down on top of a grassy mesa. They peered over the top. Below them the Sage River wound between the two steep banks. On the wide alluvial plain spread the rows of white tents of the Sage River camp. There was a lot of activity below, and the racket rose from the wide valley. Men busied themselves packing gear, currying horses, fetching water, and building up campfires.

The bulky figure of Bill O'Hagan came into view and, at his side, the quick-moving figure of Redmond O'Keefe. Between them walked Terrence O'Shaughnessey, his arms bound behind him. Well, at least the trapper was still alive, Fargo thought. But for how long? Terrence and Redmond seemed to be deep in conversation as they disappeared inside a smaller tent at the edge of the camp.

Fargo's eyes swept the lines of horses and the wagons full of supplies and came to rest on a heavy, enclosed mountain wagon. He recognized it immediately and smiled.

"Well, well," he murmured.

"What?" Oscar asked.

"That's a full load of gunpowder down there in that wagon," Fargo said, pointing it out. "A nice big explosion at just the right moment might just make an army move along." Oscar shook his head solemnly as he looked down at the gunpowder wagon.

One group of men marched up and down smartly, practicing phalanx formations. Another group was target shooting. No doubt about it. They were a bunch of disciplined professionals. Among these men were the same wary-eyed toughs he had led on the wagon train. And there were seven hundred of them. Quite an army. They would be hard to stop.

"We're too exposed here," Fargo said suddenly, glancing around. "They're bound to have patrols and lookouts posted."

"What . . . what if they catch us?" Oscar said nervously. "I don't want to get shot."

Fargo ignored him as his sharp gaze swept the hillsides. He spotted a tall thicket of sage which covered the hillside not far away. "Let's head for that," he said, retreating from the edge of the precipice on his elbows and knees. Oscar followed awkwardly.

"Ouch!" Wyndham muttered as he crawled over the sharp rocks.

They led the three mounts slowly into the tall sage thicket. It was rough going. Wyndham's horses balked, not liking the prickly branches jabbing their ribs as they forced their way inside the brush. They found a small clearing large enough for the three horses. Fargo tethered them.

"We'll go on foot from here," he said. "Bring your camera." They struggled downhill through the sage brush with the equipment, dashing across the open spaces and taking advantage of every cover. Oscar was keeping up fairly well. Just as they emerged from the sage to make a dash across a clearing, Fargo heard the faint jangle of spurs and then men's voices nearby. He froze, pushed backward into the sage, and signaled Oscar to remain still. The men, four of them, passed by on the next ridge, riding slowly and scanning the terrain.

"One of the patrols," Fargo said quietly, grateful for the sage cover. The thicket ended at the edge of the bluff overlooking the camp. Couldn't be better, Fargo thought as he gazed down. They had a panoramic view of the camp and all the activity. Oscar could set up his camera here in the thicket, and, chances were they would escape detection. It would make a really interesting photograph, Fargo thought. Interesting to Lieutenant Norrington, anyway. He hoped.

"This will be a challenge," Oscar said thoughtfully, donning his spectacles and looking about at the ground and the camp below them. He began to unpack his equipment. He unscrewed the long legs from the camera box, setting it carefully on a cloth he placed on the ground. He crawled under the black cloth and looked through the lens, pushing the camera gradually forward until it captured the scene below. Fargo watched as Oscar began to pour the chemicals from bottles into metal trays.

"Only a few hours of daylight left," Fargo said, looking at the lengthening shadows on the western bluffs. "We're lucky it's a clear day." Oscar was so involved in his work he hardly heard. Fargo lay down and continued to watch the camp below him. After a while O'Hagan and O'Keefe left the smaller tent, walking on a slow inspection tour and ending up in the larger central tent. The photographer exposed plate after plate, a moving shape beneath the black cloth. There wasn't much he could do at the moment, Fargo thought. Just watch and wait for dark. His eyes closed and he dozed off.

Some time later Fargo awoke. The shadows of evening were filling the valley below and a peachblow haze was in the western sky where the sun had just set. He rolled over. Oscar was snoring softly. His camera was neatly packed away again. Fargo looked down at the golden fires among the white tents in the blue dusk. It was time to pay a visit, Fargo knew. He rose to his feet and then stooped over to retrieve the photographs stacked neatly on a black cloth. There was just enough light to make out the details of the photographs. In a moment he shook Oscar awake.

"Where the hell are the soldiers?" Fargo asked. "These are wonderful pictures of the camp, but it doesn't look like anybody's there!" Oscar rubbed his eyes, sleepily.

"I'm sorry," he said. "They were moving too fast for the shutter, so they disappeared. People have to hold still for a while for the camera to pick them up. Otherwise they just become a blur or disappear."

"Damn," Fargo said. He hadn't thought of that. He held the photos close to his face, peering at them in the fading light. Still, the photographs did show the camp. And the corral full of tethered horses showed up as well as a few figures of men standing guard or sitting down. Well, it was the best they could do, Fargo thought. He hoped it would convince Norrington.

"Look, it was hard enough to develop those things out here in the bushes," Oscar added. "We're lucky to get anything at all."

"I guess," Fargo said, studying them again.

"Got anything to eat?" Oscar asked. "I'm starving." Fargo realized how hungry he was. But now that it was nearly dark, he needed to get a move on.

"There's pemmican in my saddlebag. I'm going down into camp to pay a visit." Fargo saw Oscar's look of surprise.

"Down there?" The fear sounded again in Oscar's voice.

"Terrence O'Shaugnessey won't last long in the same camp with Bill O'Hagan. And I'm going down to get him out. Why don't you get back to the horses," Fargo said. "You might be safer there."

"I think I'd rather stay here," Oscar said slowly. "I want to watch in case something happens to you."

Fargo set off, moving back from the edge of the bluff and then making his way slowly and quietly through the sage which crept down the side of the long ridge. When the sage petered out, he dashed across a wide plain, jumping into a small ravine which he followed downward toward the river. When it grew too shallow to hide him, he sighted a line of cotton-woods which stretched almost into the camp.

It took almost an hour to come to the last tree. Two patrols had passed by, the second one so close that Fargo had shinnied up the trunk, pressing himself against bark. The bare branches did not afford much cover, but he had less chance of being spotted in the tree than on the flat ground.

When all was clear, he eased himself down and crawled forward, taking advantage of every dip in the ground, every log, every low bush, while avoiding the snowy patches on which he could be easily seen and where he would leave suspicious tracks. Finally, he reached the perimeter of the camp and paused. It was completely dark. The campfires burned deep gold, and all the men were gathered around them. Ahead of him was the tent he had last seen Terrence enter. Fargo eased forward by inches, listening. There was no sound.

He thought fast. Puckering his lips, he made the sound of the saw-whet owl, the same signal he used at the deserted barn the night of the meeting. There was a long silence. Fargo waited. From inside came the answering call, very low. Fargo crept next to the canvas wall. The army issue tents had entrance flaps only in the front. He peered around the tent. There was no one in sight. Bending down and drawing his Colt, he ran around to the front and ducked inside.

Just as he had suspected, Terrence O'Shaugnessey sat bound on a blanket in the middle. It was dark in the tent.

"Fargo!" Terrence said. "Never expected to see you alive again! I thought Maureen got her hands on you."

"Takes more than an angry woman to kill me," Fargo said with a grin. "I'm getting you out of here." He began to untie the ropes binding Terrence's hands.

"No, wait," the trapper said.

"They're planning to kill you."

"I know," O'Shaugnessey said. "But not until I've been of use to them. Redmond's taken control. He wants to make his own decisions about how to invade Canada. O'Hagan still doesn't trust me, but I spent most of the afternoon convincing Redmond I might be an ally. In exchange for my life. I told him about a secret old Indian trail I know of—right between Longbow Coulee and McIver's Gap—that will take them right where they want to be. I even located the general area on their maps." Fargo smiled in the darkness.

"What would you have done if I hadn't come along?" Fargo asked.

"I thought that the cliff might kill some of them," Terrence said slowly. "At best, I would have slipped away. At worst, they'd have killed me." Fargo nodded to himself in the darkness.

"Do you think they'll fall for it?" he asked.

"More like fall over it," Terrence answered.

"If we can just get the troop running forward blindly," Fargo muttered, voicing his thoughts. "Otherwise, they'll catch on to what's happening to the men in front and they'll halt."

"I told Redmond that, for secrecy's sake, the troop should march at night," O'Shaugnessey added. "He's convinced."

"Good," Fargo said. "And with any luck we'll have some help from up north." He quickly told Terrence about the photographs of the camp and his plan to talk to Lieutenant Norrington again. "Even though there are just a hundred British soldiers, it might be enough if O'Hagan's army believes they're outnumbered."

"Hmmm. It's risky, isn't it?" Terrence muttered.

"It's the only chance we've got," Fargo answered. He heard footsteps approaching the tent, and he stiffened, but they passed by. "I'd better get going. See you tomorrow night at the cliff." He gagged Terrence

141

and looked out the front flap. No one in sight. Fargo ducked around the tent again and began to make his painstaking way back up to the sage stand at the top of the bluff. It was near midnight when, tired and hungry, he came upon Oscar still perched on the overlook. Below, the campfires were dim red embers, and nothing moved in the camp.

"I'm back," he said softly. Oscar jumped into the air.

"Goodness, gracious!" he said. "I didn't hear you sneaking up."

"I found Terrence," Fargo said, taking the photographs from Oscar and tucking them inside his buckskin jacket. They began to make their way back through the thicket to the horses. "And now, I'm riding to Canada. You can go back to New Dublin, if you want."

"No," Oscar said. "I been doing some thinking. I'm going to hang around. You and Terrence might need me again. You know—for escape ideas or photographs or something." As they pushed their way through the thick sage, Fargo smiled in the darkness, noting the new firmness in the photographer's voice. "I mean, I sure don't want to get shot at. But if I accidentally ride into one of their patrols tomorrow morning, I'm going to tell them I'm looking for scenery to photograph. Then, when they take me into camp, I can innocently volunteer to do their portraits or document whatever it is they're up to."

"Sounds like a good plan," Fargo said. "But there'll be a lot of shooting when they get to Canada."

"I'll just try to stay out of the way," Oscar said. The three horses were waiting quietly, nosing the ground between the patches of snow for dried grasses. Fargo fished some pemmican and beef jerky out of his saddlebag, pocketing some and handing the rest to Oscar. "That'll hold you for a while."

"I've got something for you," Oscar said. "You

know, in case anything happens." Fargo heard the note of fear in Oscar's voice. Wyndham patted the front of his coat and then felt about in his pocket, pulling out a small photograph and handing it to Skye. He held it flat to catch the starlight and saw dimly his own figure standing and Bernadette seated in front.

"It's the only copy," Oscar said.

"Thanks," said Fargo, pocketing it. "See you up north."

Fargo led the pinto pony uphill through the sage, and at the edge of the thicket he paused, scanning the top of the mesa, which was dim in the moonless night. Finally, satisfied that no one was near, he mounted and set off, keeping to the edges of brush and the dark sides of the hills. After a couple of miles, he relaxed and put the spur to the Ovaro. He galloped across the wide plain, heading northward into the night.

"These photographs prove absolutely nothing," Lieutenant Norrington said, his red mustache twitching. "Nothing!" He tossed them onto the table before him.

Fargo felt the anger burn in him. The man was a fool. He glanced up at the young corporal standing nearby with a sergeant and a few regulars. The corporal winced slightly, obviously discomfited by Norrington's skepticism, and the men looked at one another, shaking their heads. They shared Fargo's assessment of their commander.

"You asked for proof. This is the best I can bring you," Fargo said. "The photographer and I risked our lives to get them."

"Hmmm . . ." Norrington said to himself. He glanced down at the scattered prints again. "I will grant that the land surrounding this camp looks like the territory south of here, across the border. Quite a lot, in fact. And the evidence of those tents and horses can't be denied. And I understand your explanation that the moving soldiers wouldn't show up in the photograph. But damnit man, you're asking me to believe you—a complete stranger—coming to tell me a preposterous tale of invasion!"

"Then think about explaining to your superiors how you had intelligence of the invasion plans, but chose to ignore them," Fargo said. Out of the corner of his eye, he saw the corporal vigorously nodding his head in agreement. "Think about explaining that when Bill O'Hagan and Redmond O'Keefe are holding your province hostage."

"Redmond O'Keefe?" repeated the lieutenant, his voice somber. "I know all about his treason in Ireland. Is O'Keefe mixed up in this?"

"Not only mixed up in it, but leading the invasion." Fargo paused to let that sink in. "Look, Lieutenant, it's only one day's delay to march southward and check out my story."

Fargo saw the hesitation still in Norrington's face. A spineless idiot, he thought to himself.

"But . . . but I have my orders . . ." Norrington muttered, half to himself.

"Then I'll be only too happy to repeat this conversation at your court martial," Fargo snapped, turning away. He stalked toward the Ovaro and was about to mount. The goddamn British military, he thought. No wonder we won in '76.

"You there!" Norrington called out after him. "Wait!" Behind him he heard the lieutenant's footsteps approaching. Fargo ignored him and swung up into the saddle, then looked down as Norrington approached.

"Is . . . is Redmond O'Keefe really leading this pack of Bogtrotters?" Norrington looked up at him, squinting in the sun.

"I've already told you that," Fargo said. Norrington was coming around, he realized. Well, let him sweat it a little. "I'm wasting words talking to you." Fargo lifted the reins across the Ovaro, but before he could flap them Norrington cut in.

"All right, all right," the lieutenant said. "We'll march south one day to check out this ridiculous tale."

"What's the point?" Fargo asked, edging his words with sarcasm. "There are seven hundred of them and one hundred of you." Norrington blanched slightly, but recovered quickly.

"I remember you saying that," Norrington said, his voice suddenly clipped. Fargo had gotten to his pride. "Nevertheless, it is my duty to repel any invading rabble. But we'll need a superior plan." Fargo relaxed in the saddle. Well, they might be able to pull this off after all, he thought.

"I have that all figured out," Fargo said, smiling down at the lieutenant. "But first, do you have a jacket I could borrow? One of those English cutaways, short in front? Dark-colored. And a vest?"

"I certainly do," sputtered the lieutenant, "but whatever would you need that for?"

"Let's just say I'd like to dress for the occasion," Skye answered with a smile. He dismounted. "Now, let's have a look at your maps."

Fargo watched as the sun sank over the mountains in the far distance. He pulled at the lieutenant's dress jacket, which was a little tight across his broad shoulders, and he adjusted the wide black hat on his head. In the dim light and in clothes borrowed from Norrington, he'd pass for Redmond. If he needed to.

For the hundredth time his eyes scanned the distance from the edge of the wood where he stood beside his pinto across the broad meadow to the opposite edge of the dark forest on the other side. Down the center of the grassy clearing ran a broad track, partially overgrown, but still recognizable as an old, hardly used trail. In the hours after he arrived with the British unit, he had scouted it out thoroughly. Ahead, the track sloped upward between the trees, which hid cliffs on either side, becoming gradually higher and higher, the path itself ending suddenly in a huge precipice.

Past this point where the British unit hid in the woods, there was no way forward except off the cliff— at the end of the trail or through the fringe of trees on either side to the precipice. And that was the magic of Estipah-Siki-Kini-Kots. Fargo thought gratefully of Ravenbeak. He'd thank him if he ever ran into him again. That is, if it worked.

A movement caught his eye. The lieutenant had emerged from the woods on his horse and rode out into the open, approaching the trail. He signaled Fargo to join him. The fool, Fargo thought, also for the hundredth time. He rode out swiftly.

"The New Dubliners might be along any minute," Fargo called out. "Stay back in the woods."

"My men are patrolling the area," said Norrington with an airy wave of his hand. "They'll signal us when the army is approaching." Fargo thought about how easy it had been to ride into the unit's camp up north. He didn't have much confidence in Norrington's lookouts. "Now," the lieutenant continued, "I just wanted to make sure of the signal to attack."

"Okay," Fargo said. "Let's go over it again. Keep your men in the trees." How many times would he have to tell Norrington how the plan would work, he wondered. "When we see the end of the column go by, I'll ride out to join them. In the dusk they'll think I'm Redmond O'Keefe. I hope. I'll try to find a way to ignite the gunpowder wagon. When it explodes, the troops will be in confusion and you attack the rear, driving them before you. I'll lead them forward toward the cliff." And, he hoped, keep from being pushed over by the stampede.

"Righto," Norrington said, as if hearing it all for

the first time. "A really ripping plan! They'll never know what hit them!" Fargo heard hoofbeats along the trail, and he glanced up into the dusk. "Here come my men," Norrington added.

Fargo waited as the sounds drew nearer, the riders hidden by the curve in the trail. Four men. Riding fast. They came into view and advanced a few paces before reining in. Fargo swore. The round form of O'Hagan and two of his men, along with Terrence O'Shaugnessey sat astride their horses. The British lookouts had failed. Once again.

"What the hell?" Fargo heard O'Hagan say, even from the distance of a hundred strides. He knew what O'Hagan saw . . . the tall, dark bearded man dressed as Redmond O'Keefe talking to a group of scarlet-coated British soldiers. Their reaction was instantaneous. O'Hagan and his two men wheeled about immediately and galloped back down the trail. O'Shaugnessey hesitated for a brief instant, not sure whether to join Fargo or retreat. Then he followed O'Hagan.

"Keep your men in the woods," Fargo called to Norrington, as he put his spur to the Ovaro and followed. The pinto moved with powerful strides under him, the dark edges of the forest suddenly a passing blur. He rounded the curve, gaining on them. O'Hagan must not make it back to alert the approaching army. The British unit was outnumbered seven to one. Without the element of surprise, the British would be badly beaten.

Fargo drew his Colt and took slow aim at one of the men, squeezing the trigger. The impact of the bullet made the man half spin in his saddle. He fell and his mount slowed. Fargo passed the loping horse and fallen rider in a flash. Ahead, O'Hagan and the other man dug into their horses. Terrence dropped back, joining Fargo. O'Shaugnessey drew his rifle and signaled that he would take out O'Hagan.

O'Hagan's second man turned in his saddle and fired backward. Fargo ducked, hearing the bullet scream just beside his head. Still hunched down and hanging over beside the neck of the Ovaro, he took aim and fired, catching the second one in the chest as he turned to fire again. The second man slumped over and rolled slowly off the galloping horse, dragged along by one foot still in the stirrup. They gained on O'Hagan. Terrence fired and O'Hagan jolted out of his saddle, clutching his shoulder. He was winged.

Bill turned to see them coming closer. He drew and fired, the shot going wide. Then he suddenly pulled his bay over toward the edge of the forest. He was going to try to escape through the trees, Fargo realized. O'Hagan plunged into the dense wood, and they followed. Fargo's Ovaro smartly dodged the trees, finding footing among the rocks and pine needles.

Fargo and Terrence kept low as the branches swept in. They were gaining on O'Hagan. Fargo drew his Colt and took aim as Bill turned in his saddle, pistol raised. Just then, his bay galloped beneath the low branches of a thick pine and Fargo watched as a thick branch caught the back of O'Hagan's neck. Even at the distance of several strides, Fargo heard the crack of O'Hagan's neck above the sound of the hoofbeats. The bay galloped forward as O'Hagan hung for a moment, suspended by the branch, his body limp, the eyes wide with surprise, the horse no longer beneath him. Then the heavy branch broke with a loud crack under the weight.

Fargo and Terrence reined in as Bill O'Hagan dropped heavily to earth, followed by the pine branch which lay across his chest. They looked through the darkness at the body of O'Hagan. Then, suddenly, with his last strength and cunning, O'Hagan raised his rifle and fired straight at O'Shaugnessey.

Terrence's face exploded with the impact and he slumped forward across the neck of his horse. Fargo aimed his pistol at O'Hagan, but he didn't move again. O'Hagan managed to kill Terrence . . . he'd won that, Fargo thought. But that would be his last victory.

Fargo swore as Terrence's body slipped off his mount and fell onto the ground. The trapper wouldn't die in vain, Fargo promised himself. He turned the pinto back toward the trail.

Three down. Six hundred and ninety-seven to go, Fargo thought. Including Redmond O'Keefe. When he came to the edge of the woods, Fargo paused and looked out to the trail, hearing the sound of the approaching army. The advance guard of the New Dublin army came into view, marching in phalanx formation with all rifles at the ready. He scanned the column, relieved not to see Redmond among them. He recognized Seamus O'Carroll and Willie O'Brien among some of the familiar faces. But where was Redmond? Fargo rode out of the woods toward them, grateful for the near darkness.

"Redmond!" one of the men shouted. "We thought you were in the rear!"

"I cut through the woods," he said. "I was scouting the trail ahead."

"What was the shooting?" another called out.

"Three Indians jumped O'Hagan and me and two others. We killed them all, but they got Bill and the other two."

"They got Bill O'Hagan?" one of the men muttered, crossing himself. "Jesus!"

Then Fargo saw some of the men look at one another questioningly. He didn't like their looks. He couldn't give them time to get suspicious. "Pass the word back—there's a good place to stop just ahead, over the top of this long hill. Let's go. And pass the word to pick up the pace!"

Fargo wheeled about and led. He heard the men start up after him. After a while he glanced back. The

149

men were charging forward, but weren't keeping pace with the Ovaro. He slowed a little to let them catch up, then more when he realized he didn't want the column to become too strung out. The lumbering supply wagons were in the rear, and he didn't want them to get too far behind. In order for the plan to work, the last men and supply wagons had to pass by the British troops hidden in the woods just as the men at the front of the column came to the cliff.

Just ahead was the curve where the British army was hiding in the woods. They hadn't come upon the two men Fargo had shot, or their horses. Somebody from the British unit had followed, he guessed, retrieving the bodies or hiding them in the woods. Somebody was thinking fast. Definitely not Norrington.

As they rounded the curve, Fargo half expected to see the red-coated lieutenant sitting in the middle of the trail. But it was empty. No British in sight. The sky above was losing the little remaining light, and the stars were coming out. So far, so good, Fargo thought.

The one problem with this plan, he realized, as they started up the slope, was that if he continued to lead the column, he would be swept over the cliff when the stampede began. Then he had an inspiration. He reined in and turned about.

"Lead on, men," he said to the front column. "The stopping point is a half mile ahead just over the top of this long rise. I'll fall back again and bring up the rear." The second problem, he thought, was running into O'Keefe again.

Fargo maintained his position as the men rode around him, a moving mass of dark shapes in the deepening night. He encouraged them as they rode by, repeating his message that the stopping place was just ahead. It certainly was, he thought to himself. Many of these men would be crowded off the cliff and die, he realized as he watched them ride by. Not all of them, by any means. But, he hoped, enough to even out the odds so that the British could capture the survivors. On the other hand, if these men didn't die tonight, then hundreds of others—innocent settlers, British subjects, and American citizens—would be slaughtered by this army as they dug into their territory and eventually expanded.

The men continued to eddy around him, and he realized that the supply wagons and the end of the column were coming around the curve. The front of the column was probably approaching the cliff up ahead. The next few moments would spell success or failure, he realized. And Redmond O'Keefe would come into view at any second. It was time to get out of sight. Just then, Fargo saw a familiar figure riding tiredly in his saddle in the very center of the column. When the rush forward started, Fargo realized, Oscar Wyndham would be right in the middle of it.

"Get this man out!" Fargo ordered in a rough voice, pointing at Oscar. "He's holding up the line." Oscar started and peered in the darkness toward Fargo. Several of the men reined in to allow Oscar to slip by them, leading the second horse with his equipment. The movement created chaos in the line, as more men slowed down to allow Oscar to pass by.

Suddenly a loud, familiar voice cut through the confusion.

"What would be holding us up here?" Redmond O'Keefe called out, as he rode up through the column. Several of the men near Fargo suddenly jumped in their saddles to see Redmond riding up from behind them and then they turned to look at Fargo. Damn, Fargo thought. He'd have to jump the gun on their plan. Or risk losing everything.

"What's going on?" one of the men shouted, looking from one to the other.

"It's a trap!" Fargo shouted. "Forward!" Fargo galloped between the lines of the columns, shouting to the men to ride forward fast. "It's a trap!" he shouted again.

The army began to surge up the hill. The men, not being able to see in the darkness, shouted and galloped, the panic spreading up the line as the noise of the confusion carried up the hill. Fargo turned in his saddle to see several figures in pursuit.

He heard Redmond O'Keefe's voice shouting for the men to stop. And then shouting for them to chase Fargo.

Where the hell was the British army, Fargo wondered. They should be pouring out of the woods by now, but there was silence from the dark forest on either side. Then he realized that the signal, the goddamn signal to attack, was to be the explosion of the gunpowder wagon. Oh, hell. And knowing Norrington, he probably would sit in the woods until he heard an explosion.

"Sonofabitch!" Fargo swore and pulled his rifle from his saddle. As the Ovaro pushed up the hill, he stood in his stirrups and half turned his long muscular body, looking back down the slope. He could still just make out the square shape of the mountain wagon at the end of the line. Fargo raised his rifle and fired, reloaded, fired, reloaded, fired, cursing again and again, his legs cramping from the effort to hold himself steady in the saddle. A shot whizzed by. Close. Damn close. Redmond no doubt. Willing to kill one of his own men for the chance to bag him. Fargo sat in the saddle again, replacing his rifle in the saddle holster. Oh, hell. If the British didn't attack, the panic would subside.

"Come on, men!" Fargo shouted again, urging them forward. Just then the hillside lit up with a sudden golden light, and the rolling boom of a gigantic explosion shook him. Fargo laughed out loud, the sound hidden in the long series of explosions, one after another after another which lit the night. Somebody got to the gunpowder wagon.

The sound of gunfire erupted from the forest behind him. The shots began to zing around on all sides as the British army fired into the back of the column and poured out of the wood, driving the men before them.

"The redcoats!" one of the men screamed. "It's an ambush!"

Fargo ducked, hugging close to the neck of the Ovaro as the bullets rained down. He pushed his mount deeper into the column as they rushed up the hill. Men were shouting in confusion and firing. Ahead, Fargo heard screams and shouts. The front of the column had reached the precipice and, in the darkness, with the rest of the troop pressing them, were helpless to stop their forward motion and were plummeting off the cliff. Fargo pushed his way to the side of the column. If he could just get off into the fringe of the woods, he might save himself and his horse.

"Forward! Keep going!" Fargo shouted to the men. They continued to surge forward on the trail, panicking in the darkness. Just as he reached the edge of the trees, above the din of battle and confusion, Fargo heard a wailing cry of rage. He turned.

"I'll be sending you to hell!" Redmond O'Keefe shrieked, sitting on his horse, his rifle raised. Fargo slipped from his pinto just as Redmond pulled the trigger. The bullet zinged overhead as Fargo plunged into the thick woods, leaving the Ovaro behind. If he could lead Redmond away from his men and then jump him . . .

The trees were close together with thick underbrush and rocky terrain. He'd have to watch his step. The cliff was nearby, and it was completely dark under the trees. Fargo ducked behind a pine tree and looked out. He heard nothing in the fringe of wood, but the echoes of the shouts of the men and screams from the direction of the trail's end. Fargo waited for a moment. Still, he heard nothing. Then he felt someone behind him. Damn! He whirled and the rifle exploded, the report deafening him as he felt the sudden burning pain as the Colt was torn from his grasp.

Fargo leapt forward and to the side as a second shot exploded, splitting the air where he had been a moment before. He hit the rocky ground and rolled once toward Redmond, hitting his knees and knocking him to the ground.

His right hand was useless, he found, numbed by the impact of Redmond's rifle blast. Damn, he felt nothing below his wrist. But he seized Redmond's rifle with his left hand, twisting it out of the man's grasp and tossing it away and delivered two hard blows using his unfeeling hand as a heavy club. Redmond kneed him, and the pain exploded inside him as his one-hand grip loosened for a moment and Redmond twisted free, crawling away. Fargo leapt to his feet and vaulted after the retreating figure, rolling with him in the darkness over the rocks and through the underbrush until suddenly he felt the ground give way beneath his shoulder and he saw the open sky and stars above him. They were at the edge of the cliff.

Fargo released his hold on Redmond and grasped at a small tree to stop his forward motion. The young sapling bent as he began to slide off the precipice. He felt O'Keefe scrambling for a hold too. Fargo lashed out, kicking at Redmond, but his foot flew wide into space. He hung, dangling over the cliff, holding on to the sapling. He felt the vibration of its roots tearing slowly out of the soil, pulled by his weight. Goddamn. And Redmond O'Keefe lay on the cliff just above him.

Fargo tried to climb up, using his numbed right hand, but the fingers wouldn't close. Redmond's face appeared above him, looking down.

"You're a dead man," Redmond said in a hoarse voice. "You can't stop us." Fargo thought fast. If he could keep Redmond talking . . .

"Give it up, O'Keefe," Fargo barked. "O'Hagan's dead. Your whole army's gone over the cliff."

"But I'm still alive," breathed Redmond.

"The British army's coming up the hill," Fargo said. "You won't be for long."

"I'll do just fine," O'Keefe said. "In another few minutes I'll be walking out of this woods to tell that British commander that I just kicked Redmond O'Keefe over the cliff."

Fargo gritted his teeth. That sonofabitch, he thought. And Norrington would fall for it too. The lieutenant would never figure out that O'Keefe was only pretending to be Fargo. And then O'Keefe would get away. Fargo felt the rage boil in him. Once again he tried to use his right hand, but it was no good. He waved his legs, trying to get a foothold in the cliff, but his boots slipped. The sapling creaked.

Above him, Redmond reached down and began to push at the roots of the tree, back and forth, loosening it more as Fargo hung in space. The tree became looser and Fargo felt it slip. In another moment he would fall to his death. Goddamn useless hand, Fargo thought, beating it in frustration against the rock. Suddenly, he had an idea and jammed the paralyzed hand into a crevice, turning the wrist so the hand held his weight. Just as the sapling tore loose, Fargo let go of it and grabbed on to a pointed rock. Above him he heard Redmond swear.

Fargo pulled his right hand out of the crevice and jammed it in higher as he felt Redmond trying to pry the fingers of his left hand free from the rock. But it was too late. He felt hope, fury, and strength flowing through his body as he pulled himself up to the top of the cliff. Just as his head cleared the top, he sighted Redmond, ready to kick him, and at the last instant he ducked. O'Keefe missed, and Fargo scrambled over the top, just as Redmond lost his footing. He slipped and fell onto Fargo. Fargo felt Redmond's hands clutching at him for a hold. But in a moment he bounced off, plunging over the side of the precipice. Redmond O'Keefe made no sound as he fell to his death.

After a moment Fargo rolled onto his back and lay in the darkness, listening to the sounds of the battle. There were no more sounds of screaming men falling to their death. They must have surrendered. There was the pop of gunfire coming up the hill, not far away—the British—scouring the woods and driving the last of the men before them. Fargo got wearily to his feet, cradling his right hand. Well, all the fingers were still there, he noted. But he felt the warm slickness of blood and the beginnings of the return of sensation. Hell, he thought, as the hand began to throb. He'd be shooting with his left for a while.

Fargo retraced his steps and retrieved his Colt. He found the pinto waiting for him just inside the periphery of the woods. In the starlight Fargo could see the British soldiers efficiently rounding up O'Hagan's men, who had surrendered completely, throwing down their rifles. Fargo stepped forward toward the trail. He walked toward a group of O'Hagan's men standing docilely in a tight group. Fargo recognized Norrington and his corporal sitting on their horses, as he neared.

"Redmond!" one of the men shouted. "We lost our fight. Give us some words, Redmond!"

"Redmond! Redmond!" the other men took up the cry. Several of the British soldiers started forward to capture him, but Fargo stopped them with a raised hand. He removed Norrington's jacket, vest and hat slowly, tossing them to the lieutenant. Fargo retrieved his hat and jacket from his saddlebag, donned them, mounted the pinto, and turned to address the men who had fallen silent in despair and confusion.

"Redmond O'Keefe is dead," Fargo said, his words ringing out in the darkness to the assembled men. "So is Bill O'Hagan. And so is your conspiracy. You still have your town. But call it something new, something fitting. Something that looks forward to the future and not back to the past. You've come to America to find a new life. So don't bring old wars and old hates with you. Leave them where they belong. Back in Ireland."

The men were silent.

"I commend you," Norrington said grandly, saluting him. "In fact, all of the empire of Great Britain commends your . . ."

Fargo didn't wait to hear more, but turned and galloped down the hill. At the bottom he saw the horse loaded with the camera equipment. He reined in and looked about for Oscar. He dismounted and joined a group of British soldiers. They parted, and he saw the photographer lying on the ground, being tended by the unit's doctor. Oscar's eyes were closed, his face pale, and one of the lenses of his spectacles was cracked. He had been shot, the blood staining the front of his shirt.

"Oh hell," Fargo swore. "How bad is he?"

"Just the shoulder," answered the medic, holding a pair of tongs in his hand, ready to remove the bullet. "He'll be all right in a few weeks." Oscar's eyes fluttered open.

"Fargo?" he called. "I got the gunpowder wagon! I made it explode! And I got shot!" Fargo heard the unmistakable note of pride in the photographer's voice. "And you know what?" he added. "Getting shot's not that bad. It's not bad at all."

"So you set fire to the powder! You saved the day, Oscar," Fargo said. "Thanks. See you around."

There was no answer, and Fargo mounted and rode on. He didn't want to be around when the doctor started probing around in Oscar's shoulder for the bul-

157

let. Oscar would change his mind about how bad it was getting shot.

The pinto galloped past groups of captured men, lines of tethered horses, and the still smoldering ruin of the exploded gunpowder wagon. Fargo smiled to himself, imagining Wyndham finding the guts to put fire to the wagon. In another moment he was beyond the battlefield and galloping south on the open trail under the starlight.

The miles of unexplored forest and endless plains seemed to welcome him as he moved forward through the long night, eyes and ears alert to the many sounds of the night. The first pale fingers of dawn's light found him sitting tall on his pinto at the top of a bluff overlooking the wide plain and the winding Sage River below.

He pulled the photograph from his pocket and studied the faces. They looked like people he used to know, he decided. In the past. He let the photograph flutter to the grass and then turned off the trail, heading another direction, where he had never been before.

*1860, Lost Trail Pass in the
Salmon River Mountains of the
Idaho Territory, the wild land
where death could strike by arrow,
bullet, fang, or claw . . .*

He had often thought about this moment, but her words said everything, better than he could. "I waited, wondered, never stopped hoping, Fargo," she said and he nodded.

"Just couldn't get up this way till now," he said, his lake blue eyes taking in the young woman in front of him. Bonnie hadn't changed, not really, except for perhaps ten added pounds. Her medium brown hair and medium brown eyes were still part of an open, friendly face, more sweet then pretty, her smile still winsomely warm and direct. She seemed just as he had last seen her those years ago, wearing a simple shirt, tan this time, and a black skirt. But he saw the moment of anger flare in her eyes.

"And you expect I'm so glad to see you I'll just jump right into bed with you," Bonnie said.

"No," Fargo laughed. "I don't expect that."

"Then you're wrong," she said, and with one quick

motion pulled buttons open and flung the shirt aside. Bonnie's breasts were still as he'd remembered, modest yet with enough fullness to fit perfectly on her average frame, average-size tips of average pink on modest pink circles. Everything about Bonnie was average except for her open, unvarnished honesty, her unwillingness to play games. That openness had always been part of her sweet attractiveness and it was still so, he realized as her arms slid around his neck. His mouth pressed hers as she started to shed clothes, and he felt her skirt slide down and she pulled him with her onto the small but thick rug on the floor of her modest living room.

Bonnie's thighs, a little fleshier now, rose up at once to clasp around him as his hands roamed her body and his lips found one modest breast and sucked gently on the pink tip. "Yes, oh, God, Fargo . . . bring it back, bring it all back," she murmured, and her arms were around him, sliding up and down his back and her convex little belly, also a little fuller, was already rising up for him. His hand slid down onto the very curly but small *V* and felt the firm softness just below the fibrous tendrils. He touched, felt her already moistened for him, and Bonnie gave her gasping half scream and dug fingers into his back. He pressed deeper, caressed the soft lips, touched the tender places, and Bonnie's thighs opened and closed against him. "Oh, God, yes . . . so good, so good," she moaned. "So wonderful . . . so good."

Her moans grew deeper, longer as he continued to caress and stroke, and when he brought his own pulsating warmth to her, the moans changed into the tiny half-screamed gasps that come over and over and over as she pumped and rose with him, pushed and fell back with him, hurried moments, as much a plea to herself as to him until suddenly they grew in pitch and intensity and he felt her pushing frantically against him. "Yes, yes, please, please, oh God, so long, so good, oh God," Bonnie flung out. He let himself explode with her as his mouth bit gently into one modest breast and Bonnie's soft thighs clasped tighter around his waist.

He stayed with her, let the world shatter with her, and she prolonged the ecstasy as she slammed against him with her pelvis, harder and harder until, with a sudden cry, she fell back. But her arms stayed clutched around his neck, holding his mouth against her breasts. "Oh, Jesus, oh, God," she murmured into his cheek. "So good, so great, just the way it was, the way I remembered." Her hands came against the sides of his face. "It was always special with you, Fargo, always special."

"And you still don't play games," he smiled.

"No, not with you," she said.

"Not with anyone, I'll wager," he said, and her smile was almost rueful.

"That's true. I can't. It's not part of me. I do or I don't. I will or I won't," she said. "It's been mostly won't, but I'm sure you realized that."

"I wish I could stay longer," he said.

"I'll have to make whatever time we have last me till next time," Bonnie said, and she curled herself tightly against him. He heard the sound of her steady breathing in minutes. She always slept soundly as a baby afterward, he remembered, and woke up hungry for more. He lay back, cradled her against him as he smiled. It was always nice when memories held up to time. He sound himself thinking of the last time he had lain like this with Bonnie.

With her open, honest sweetness, he had already developed a special fondness for her. She was trying to make a small dry-goods store pay in a grubby little town in Utah while fighting off the advances of Banker Jethroe, the most powerful man in town. That night flooded back over him as vividly as if it had been yesterday. He was sliding from Bonnie's sleeping form in the big bed to go into the kitchen and draw some water. He walked silently on bare feet, his powerful body naked in the dim light of a kitchen candle. He was drinking deeply of the water when he heard the front door burst open, and when he rushed into Bonnie's room, the heavy figure of Banker Jethroe was already on top of her, punching her as he pushed her legs open.

Fargo moved with long, silent strides and yanked the man up, flung him halfway across the room and Banker Jethroe's heavy figure crashed on the floor. The man pushed to his feet, mean and drunk, Fargo saw, his heavy-featured face flushed. He rushed, drew one arm back to swing, and Fargo's whistling left hook caught him on the side of the jaw. He staggered backward, fell, shook his head, and looked up as his eyes cleared. "She's through in this town, mister," the man said as he rose. "She's through and you're dead."

"Get out before I break you in little pieces," Fargo said. Out of the corner of his eye he saw that Bonnie had flung her robe on and rushed to a dresser against the far wall. Banker Jethroe came at him again, his words thick-tongued.

"Let's see you do it," he snarled, and Fargo cursed silently as he took a step forward, his hands ready to lash out when the man yanked the gun from his pocket, a Sharps four-barreled Derringer, a deadly weapon at close range, the rotating striker on the hammer firing the barrels in rotation. Fargo halted, suddenly aware of his nakedness. He saw Jethroe's finger tightening on the trigger, winced, and the room exploded with the shot, far too loud for the Derringer.

His glance snapped to Bonnie and saw the big Remington-Beals with its seven-inch barrel in her hands. Banker Jethroe lay on the floor, his heavy mid-section suddenly turned red. Fargo stepped past the man and took the revolver from Bonnie's hands.

"Oh, God, what do we do?" she breathed.

"I get dressed," Fargo said as he started to pull on clothes.

"There's no hiding this. He's a prominent man," Bonnie said, staring at the lifeless figure.

"Was a prominent man," Fargo said, putting the revolver atop the dresser. "Everyone knows he was bothering you. You told me that." Bonnie nodded. "He burst in, found us together, and tried to kill you. I had to shoot him."

"You? No, I did it. I'll say so," Bonnie said, and he took her by the shoulders, turned her to face him.

"You have to go on living in this town. I don't. I'll go my way. I shot him. We'll leave it like that," he told her. "I'll go fetch the sheriff, and he can clear this formerly prominent man out of your bedroom."

"I won't let you take the blame for me," Bonnie said.

"Self-defense. It'll be our word against his and he won't be saying much," Fargo said. "You stay just the way you are till I get back." He hurried from the small house, found the sheriff's office, and woke the man up in his living quarters in the back. He told the sheriff the story he and Bonnie had agreed upon as he walked with the man to Bonnie's place.

"Self-defense, you say," the sheriff muttered.

"That's right," Fargo nodded and saw the sheriff wince. "Something wrong with that?" Fargo asked.

"Plenty," the sheriff said. "I've always liked Bonnie. I'm real sorry about this, but Banker Jethroe was an important man in town. He may be dead, but his influence isn't."

"Meaning what exactly?" Fargo asked, peering hard at the sheriff. He seemed a man who was honestly pained for Bonnie.

"We'll go into that later," the sheriff said. "But enough folks heard Bonnie say she'd kill Jethroe if he kept bothering her."

"Damn," Fargo swore softly.

"Exactly," the sheriff said.

"But I'm the one who shot him. He was going to kill me," Fargo said.

"You can tell your story when the time comes," the sheriff said. Fargo swore again, silently this time as they reached Bonnie's house and entered. Bonnie sat at the edge of the bed and rose as Fargo stepped into the room with the sheriff. "Hello, Bonnie," the sheriff said quietly. "Your friend here told me what happened. You'd be backing up his story, I take it."

"Yes," Bonnie said, swallowing, and the sheriff gazed down at the still figure of Banker Jethroe, then turned to Fargo and put his hand on the Colt in Fargo's holster. Fargo's fingers closed around the man's wrist instantly. "I'd like a look at your gun, mister," the sheriff said calmly and waited, his eyes meeting Fargo's gaze. " 'Less you've some reason why I shouldn't," he said.

Fargo grimaced inwardly as he realized that to refuse would be an admission. He unclasped his fingers and the sheriff drew the Colt, spun the chamber. His eyes narrowed. "Six-shot revolver, six bullets in it," he said, raised the barrel of the gun to his nose, and sniffed. "This gun hasn't been fired in the last twenty minutes," he said and stepped back, his eyes sweeping the room to halt at the pistol atop the dresser. He stepped to it, flipped the chamber open, and his face took on a pained grimace as he turned to Bonnie. "Want to tell me anything, girl?" he asked.

"I didn't say I shot him with my gun," Fargo put in quickly.

"I shot him," Bonnie said quietly, and she looked at Fargo. "I won't let you take the blame for it." she said.

"Dammit, Bonnie," Fargo said.

"He was going to kill Fargo," Bonnie said. "He had the Derringer pointed right at him."

"Under the law, that doesn't make it self-defense for you, Bonnie," the sheriff said.

"She came to my defense," Fargo said. "He was going to attack her."

"That'll be up to a jury to decide," the sheriff said. "You dress, Bonnie. I'll wait outside. I have to take you in." He motioned to Fargo, who stepped from the house with him.

"There's no reason for her to sit in jail," Fargo said.

"Can't let her stay free. Got to protect my job," the man said. "Remember what I said about Banker Jethroe's influence still alive? A jury we call will be made up of townsfolk, and the bank holds loans and mortgages on most everybody who'll sit on that jury. The rest of the bank's trustees won't take kindly to a jury letting go the woman that killed their president. They could call in every note and loan, and everybody will know that."

"You're saying they'll feel they have to convict her." Fargo frowned.

"I'm telling you the facts of human nature, mister," the sheriff said. "I know Jethroe was a bastard, but what I know won't count."

"Thanks for being honest," Fargo said as Bonnie came from the house. He walked in silence beside her to the jail, two small cells alongside the sheriff's office with a guard sitting in an outside room.

"Cell one," the sheriff told the guard, who ushered Bonnie into the first small cell. She offered Fargo a wan smile as he cursed silently.

"I'll be by in the morning," he told her and walked outside with the sheriff.

"You can visit her any time you like," the sheriff said. "Early morning, late night, whenever you want." Fargo's eyes peered at the sheriff. The man's face showed no emotion, yet Fargo had the distinct feeling he was doing more than spelling out visiting hours.

"What if they convict her and she escapes?" Fargo slid at the man.

"I'd have to send out wanted flyers for her as an escaped murderess," the sheriff said. "Of course, if she escaped before a trial, she'd only be wanted for questioning. I wouldn't be sending out flyers for that."

Fargo forced himself not to smile as he adopted the sheriff's bland demeanor. "Naturally. No conviction, she can't be wanted for a crime," he said.

"Naturally," the sheriff nodded.

"See you around," Fargo said as he strode off. He took the Ovaro, spent the night bedded down outside of town, and paid his first visit to Bonnie in the morning. "You can't stay. It could go badly," he told her in a whispered exchange.

"Doesn't seem I've much choice," she said.

"More than you think. What would you be taking with you if you were leaving here?" he asked.

"My clothes and my money," Bonnie said.

"The money in the bank?"

"No. I took it out. I couldn't stand going there anymore and having to see Jethroe every time. It's buried under the floor in the kitchen," Bonnie told him.

"I'll be back tonight," he said. She was frowning

when he left, the unsaid things racing through her mind. It was late that night when he returned. She stood at the bars, no frown this time but a tiny smile edging her lips. She watched in silence as he took the guard's gun and tied the man up securely, then let her out of the cell. "I've all your things and a horse out back," he said. "Where do we go?"

"North, I've some friends in Wyoming. They'll help me get started again," she said.

"North it is," he said.

The pictures snapped off in his mind and he looked at Bonnie's form beside him, still asleep in his arms. Her friends had taken her in, and from there she'd found her way to the place she was now. She'd reached him by post with that news, the last letter over a year ago, and he'd found her as content as she'd sounded then. The job, taking care of the books for a small gold-mining operation, seemed to be to her liking, and he was happy for her. Bonnie deserved a run of happiness. Not because she'd saved his life once, but because she was basically a good person.

He smiled down at her as she stirred and opened her eyes, and he saw the instant message in them. Her mouth came up to press against his, the message given tangible form, and almost at once she was pressing a soft, modest breast to his lips. The night grew warm again with her flesh and her hungering desire, and he was spent and more than satisfied when she curled up against him once again, her last, lingering scream of pleasure still hanging in the air. Later, when the dawn woke them both, she brought him a mug of coffee and sat cross-legged on the bed beside him, the tan shirt hardly concealing her soft-fleshed body.

"Tell me about this boss of yours, this Jim Gibson.

He was so damn excited when I showed up looking for you," Fargo said.

"Yes, I'm sure he was. You've a reputation, you know, Fargo," Bonnie reminded him.

"He said he had to talk to me, and I told him not till I'd seen you. I know he'll be waiting come sunup," Fargo said.

"Jim Gibson is a strong man. He runs his mine with a strong hand. But he's fair. I've seen that," Bonnie said. "Then he had a real tragedy a few months back. It's changed him, made him harder, more obsessed. I know that's what he wants to talk to you about."

"Go on," Fargo said as she paused.

"I'd rather he tell you," Bonnie said. "Listen to him. I hope you can help him. He'll pay you anything you ask, I'm sure."

Fargo made a face. "I've a job waiting. Bill Bannister in Montana wants me to trail blaze a herd for him," he said. "I'd stay longer with you otherwise."

"Hear him out. I'm sure when he saw you, it was better than finding a new strike for him," Bonnie said.

"I'll listen, for you," Fargo said and received a long, slow kiss for his answer.

"Can you stay another night?" Bonnie asked. He nodded and Bonnie swung happily from the bed, the shirt flying up to show her very round little rear. "See you then," she said, hurrying off to bathe and dress. He lay in the bed, let her finish, and heard her leave before he rose, bathed and pulled on clothes, and stepped from the little house. The mine stretched out in front of him, the low-roofed wooden building that was the office a hundred yards on, and beyond it, the wooden sluices and long Toms that ran down from the dark entrances of the caves. He strolled to the office building, glanced in a window, and saw Bonnie at work in a small office, two heavy ledger books in front of her on a table.

Jim Gibson greeted him as he entered and took him into another room with two chairs and a table. "Been waiting. Bonnie told me you'd be coming by," Gibson said. He had a square face, graying hair, Fargo took note, a strong, lined face and the eyes of a man who had met the world and won, most of the time. In Gibson's dark blue orbs he saw the pain of bitterness. "Bonnie told me about you over the last few years, how you two had a special relationship," the man said. "And how she'd given up that you'd ever get this way."

"Finally managed it." Fargo smiled.

"Thank God," Jim Gibson said fervently. "You'll be my last hope. And the best one."

"For what?"

"For finding my son, Josh," Gibson said.

"He's lost?"

"It's not as simple as that," Jim Gibson said and gestured to a chair as he paced the small room. "Josh was not only my son, he was my partner and my right hand. It was his idea and it was working until something went wrong."

"Whoa. Back up some," Fargo said.

"Yes, I'm sorry," Gibson said and drew a deep breath before he began again. "The main road north circles around to Missoula. It's a damn magnet for every band of thievin' gunslingers. They hit stages, payroll wagons, gold shipments, mail riders, everything and anything. We kept losing our gold shipments when Josh got this idea. He'd take the gold in saddle-bags, alone, through the mountains. No varmints would look for a man riding alone through the mountains with nothing to draw attention to him. It worked, over and over. I'd send dummy shipments they'd attack and go off cussing while Josh would be taking the gold through the mountains, the heart of the Bitterroot Range."

"But something went wrong," Fargo offered.

"He never came back from his last trip."

"They caught on and drygulched him?"

"No, we'd have found him then. Besides, at the time he disappeared, they had attacked three stages on the main road. Something happened to Josh, but they didn't do it. I can't go on without knowing what happened to him or whether he's still alive. I don't sleep maybe three hours a night."

"When did he disappear?" Fargo asked.

"Two months ago."

"Two months is a very cold trail." Fargo frowned.

"I know you've done colder," Jim Gibson said.

"What makes you think he might still be alive?" Fargo questioned.

"I don't know, but there was a man came to me, Roy Coulter. He lives in the mountains and said he knew what happened to Josh. He wouldn't say if Josh was alive. He wouldn't say anything more unless I paid him. I decided he was just trying to get money out of me and he didn't know anything. I refused to pay him and he left. Later, I wondered if I'd made a mistake about Roy Coulter and I went searching for him."

"You didn't find him," Fargo said.

"No, but those damn mountains are made for hiding," Gibson said. "I tried to get the army to help me."

"The army?" Fargo frowned.

"They have a small garrison at the foot of the Beaverhead Range where some families have settled in. They were useless. They didn't even do much looking," the man said darkly.

"I'm sorry for what's happened, but I'm afraid I can't help. I'm due in Montana to trail blaze a new route. It's a deal all settled months ago," Fargo said.

"I'll pay you triple what they will," Gibson said.

"Sorry. I don't go back on my word," Fargo said. "I can't help you."

"You're my last hope, a chance I never thought I'd get. You're the Trailsman. I can't just let you ride away without trying to find Josh," the man said with a mixture of steel and pleading in his voice.

"God knows how long this would take. I don't have time enough. They're expecting me in Montana. I'm real sorry, but the cards just don't fall right. Maybe when I'm finished in Montana, I could swing by this way again," Fargo said.

"The trail will be even colder then, and I might be dead from exhaustion," Gibson bit out.

"It's the best I can do. I'm sorry," Fargo said.

"Goddammit," Gibson said, slamming his fist onto the table in an explosion of anger and frustration. "It's not fair, not one goddamn bit fair. You're here and you're my last chance. Not fair, dammit, not fair."

"Didn't say it was. Not a hell of a lot in life is fair," Fargo said, getting to his feet. "Sorry again," he said as he left and felt the man's eyes boring into his back as he went out the door. He felt sorry for Jim Gibson, a man plainly distraught and at the end of his tether. There was some time before he was due at Bill Bannister's, Fargo knew, but not enough for this kind of searching a cold trail. He shook away the bitterness in the man's eyes, took the Ovaro, and led the horse behind Bonnie's place, where he spent the rest of the day giving the animal a thorough currying, using the sweat scraper first, then the body brush and sponge for eyes, nostrils and lips and lastly the stable rubber. When he finished, the day was drawing to an end and the Ovaro gleamed and glistened, jet fore- and hindquarters stark against the pure white midsection. Bonnie returned, had a stew on the kettle, and he ate with her. "You're awfully quiet," he observed.

"I was hoping you'd help Jim Gibson," she said.

"I told you I was due in Montana," he reminded her. "You said to hear him out and I did."

"I know," Bonnie nodded unhappily. "I just hoped. He's so desperate and he's changed so, grown harsh and bitter, driving his men unmercifully. Everyone's aware of it."

"That's something he'll have to work out on his own." Fargo shrugged. Bonnie nodded again, cleared away the dishes, and led him into the bedroom, where she quickly excluded the rest of the world. It was only after her cries of pleasure had died away for the second time that she allowed the world to intrude. "You'll be leaving come morning, won't you?" she murmured.

"That's right," he said. "Maybe I can swing back this way when I'm finished."

"I won't wait. I won't think about it, either," she said matter-of-factly. "That only makes waiting harder." He held her against him, understanding, and she slept tight in his arms. When morning came, he slid from beside her, dressed, and paused at the door to glance back at her. She lay unmoving, apparently still fast asleep, but he wondered as he left and promised he'd try to return when the Bannister job was finished.

He took the Ovaro and set off leisurely across the low hills along the south end of the Beaverhead Range. He had been riding for a little over an hour when he spotted the four horsemen coming at a full gallop behind him. He continued on as he watched them draw closer, and he reined to a halt at a small plateau bordered by a stand of drawf maple and waited. The four riders reached him in minutes and pulled their mounts to a stop. "Jim Gibson sent us," the one man said, middle-aged with a tired face. The other three were ordinary enough, a little younger, Fargo noted, one sporting a thin mustache. "We've orders to bring you back," the older man said.

"I said all I had to say," Fargo replied. "There's no point in my going back."

The older man sounded apologetic. "We've our orders. We don't want trouble," he said.

"Me neither, so's you just go back and tell him I said I wouldn't go with you," Fargo suggested.

The man made a face. "We can't do that. He told us to bring you back the hard way if we had to."

"Then that's what you're going to have to do, gents."

JON SHARPE'S
CANYON O'GRADY
RIDES ON

HOW THE WEST WAS WON